NEW TO THE GAME

D.C. Knights- Book 1

JUNO CHASE

Electronic ISBN: 978-0-9969045-6-8

Print ISBN: 978-1-947234-20-8

Never play with the feelings of others. You may win the game, but you may lose the person for life.

—Anonymous

Contents

Chloe admired the mahogany paneled wainscoting in the congressional conference room. The expanse of the smooth reddish-brown wood was polished to a shine. Decorative scrolls and flowers embossed the chair rail. DC was a town of yin and yang. Masculine and feminine. The Washington Monument and the Reflecting Pool. Dark wood and velvet curtains.

There were so many reasons why she loved this city. The layered levels of gray intrigued her: the different shades in the cloudy skies, the black pebbles in nearly white concrete sidewalks, the massive Ionic Greek columns protecting a statue of blind Lady Justice.

There wasn't much greenery in this part of town,

but this country mouse did not want to go home. She wanted to stay, and at the end of her second year in law school at GW, Chloe did not drive sixteen-hundred-miles back to her parent's farm. Instead, she accepted an internship with the Honorable Congressman.

The very man stood at the head of the table. His book had been required reading during her first year of law school. His memoir recalled the standard American narrative that climaxed with a rise to power. He had middle-class parents who couldn't afford to pay for college.

He worked hard, joined ROTC in high school and got a full-ride scholarship. He graduated from Annapolis just in time for his first deployment to Desert Storm. After two tours, he left the Navy to go to Harvard law school. He was the editor of the school's famous law review.

His life story was an anecdote of why he truly cared about the struggle of humanity, and how he could help better everyday lives, the reasons why he decided to be in politics. He passed the bar, then ran for city council. He won and never looked back. Now, he was a Congressman. Chloe hadn't seriously considered a career in politics, but his book inspired her. He inspired her.

Lincoln Ulysses Pierce. If that wasn't a name for a president, she didn't know what was. Behind him, artwork depicting the Revolutionary war hung, adding to his powerful aura. Damn, he was good looking. He had a great physique, wide shoulders, nice biceps. His hair, salt and pepper gray. Even without speaking, charisma radiated from him. She could be attracted to him, but ... she was there to learn, to connect with people on the Hill.

Katherine O'Malley stood next to him. She was the Senior Legislative Assistant and about to start the meeting. Katherine was considered one of the best on the Hill with a reputation for being a bad ass with a good heart. The woman was unstoppable. She was exactly the kind of woman Chloe wanted to work for.

Before she met Katherine, Chloe had never even considered working as a Congressional intern. She had heard others talk about the job like it was the crown jewel to starting a career, but at the time, she was more interested in clerking for a justice. Lady Luck intervened, and she met Katherine at a bookstore signing. Then voila! She still didn't know why she had said yes to the internship, but she knew she'd made the right decision when she walked into the Cannon House Office building on her first day. This summer would definitely be interesting.

Chloe wasn't sure if she wanted to stay in politics long-term. The day-to-day seemed rough. You needed a thick skin. Don't trust anyone. That kind of work environment required a certain kind of persona, and she wasn't sure if she was that person. Her short-term goals though, were simple: be involved as much as possible with the legislative/lobbyist aspects, and increase her contact list with important names. Maybe she'd work on the Hill or work for a lobbyist? The real money was in lobbying, but to secure a job, having worked on the Hill was preferential, and in some cases, required.

She took a sip of her to-go coffee, noting 6:30 a.m. was a bit early for a meeting. In the conference room, there were eight women and herself. Another reason she wanted to work for the Congressman. He surrounded himself with smart, hard working women. He was an outspoken feminist. His famous interview with Anderson Cooper solidified his reputation. The feminist part didn't appeal to his base, but he made sure to wrap his messages in a way that mattered in the voting polls.

The meeting was not booked using email. She received an actual hand-written memo. It seemed quaint to her. Unusual and quaint. Chloe was instructed not to put the meeting online either. It was strange, but she wasn't concerned. She just assumed the oddity was how politics worked. Even so, she had grumbled in the shower that this early bird meeting better be worth it and not something dumb like email protocol. She smoothed back her hair which happened to be up in a classic French bun.

She looked around the room at the other women who choose navy blue or black. Nobody wore much color on the Hill. The overall effect made everyone look like they wore a uniform. Chloe liked her outfit, a calf length pencil gray skirt with a fitted white button down. She wore a silver lariat necklace with two stunning topaz teardrops to accentuate her neckline. To match, she picked out a pair of dark gray high heels that usually took her from an average height to the tallest woman in the room.

"Let's get to the point," said the Congressman. "We have an important event coming up in two and a half weeks, 20 days to be exact. There is a fundraiser luncheon for the Service Dogs of America in Las Vegas. They raise money to train dogs for Vets and the disabled. I've been invited as a VIP guest. Fantastic as that charity is, it is not the real reason we are meeting today. The real reason we are going to Vegas is to meet with the Donohoe family along with August Thorne and Yukika Matthews. We're forging ahead in renewables."

Chloe recognized the names immediately because she was an avid reader of Popular Science as well as Fast Company. A closet nerd. The Donohoe family was in the 1%.

During the Depression, Donohoe Senior made inexpensive but reliable car parts. His son, Jack Donohue, transformed the company into a leading automotive manufacturer. The Donohue family did well because they stayed at the forefront of new technology with scientific and computer advances. They were one of the first to invest in Internet of Things (IoT.) IoT was tech industry's shorthand term that allows the internet to be placed in mundane things like your refrigerator, or provides the mechanism for your cars to interface with home security systems and cell phones. Chloe loved the idea of her refrigerator reminding her that she needed to buy milk.

August Thorne developed insanely efficient new batteries to power vehicles and homes. Yukika Matthews was the country's foremost solar energy expert, having helped small countries to set up alternative power sources.

Chloe's skin tingled. Meeting the Donohoes, August, and Yukika was exactly the kind of connection she'd dreamed of making while being an intern. The Vegas meeting would be part of something innovative, a game changer. If she could put this gig on her resume, she would easily get into a lobbying firm. Being part of a deal like this could change the whole trajectory of her career. Chloe sat forward in her seat, her annoyance at the early morning timing gone.

The Honorable Mr. Pierce paused to sip coffee from a standard issue ceramic mug emblazoned with the House of Representatives seal. "The secret meeting, which we'll call SUNFLOWER, will take place in a to-be disclosed location. That's why this morning's meeting is off the books, we don't want any kind of electronic trail. Future meetings will be manual if needed, but certainly not required," he said with a nod to Eleanor. The other women in the room all glanced toward her. Chloe had heard of her, but they had not been introduced formally. Eleanor was in charge of IT.

"The best way to keep safe the data is no data." Eleanor responded with a direct tone. Eleanor was all about direct, she had short, almost white blonde hair and an expression which did not show any emotion.

Clearing his throat, the Congressman started again, "The purpose of the meeting is to bring together the automotive industry giant Donohoe family with innovative technology of solar and battery power. Donohoe wants to invent new hardware to support solar power in automobiles, specifically semi-trucks that haul cross-country. He wants to create new revenue sources and save money on his own shipping fuel. Our job is to write legislation to support new jobs and generate financial incentives for our base." He paused for a moment, sat down in his chair and put on his glasses. "That covers my side. Madeline, take it from here."

"Absolutely sir. I'll introduce the team," Madeline said. She brushed back strands of her auburn hair and pushed up her sleeves. "Most of you know each other, but we need to ramp Chloe up. She's been here a week, but due to crazy schedules, this is the first opportunity to meet her. She is our newest intern, a second-year George Washington law student, and brought on board to support Katherine. Everyone, this is Chloe Cassell."

When the women turned to look at her, most of

them smiled, except Eleanor. Chloe smiled in return. Even though these women were renowned for being tough, she felt a sense of solidarity with them. She was one of the team.

Madeline took a drink of her lemon water. She looked like a model, tall and lean. Her wavy auburn hair was shoulder length. She had a necklace on. The pendant was a fencer in lunge position with a diamond stud at the hilt of the sword. Madeline caught her eye and smiled before continuing. "Katherine will be working on the bill itself with one of the foremost environmental lawyers in the country. I'll be handling the optics. Cheyenne will help me out, and Opal will work directly with Link. Opal will also be coordinating logistics and schedules for both the charity luncheon and SUNFLOWER. Lizbeth will be working the Committee angles. Chloe will help her out too, as needed. Eleanor will be running all the IT and background research for SUNFLOWER. She'll let us know specific protocols to assure this project goes off without a hitch."

Chloe sat back and glanced around the table to get herself organized. Katherine law. Madeline PR. Eleanor IT. Cheyenne works mainly as Madeline's assistant. Opal was Lincoln's assistant. Lizbeth committees. Chloe didn't have a photographic memory, but she used mnemonic tricks which had served her well over the years.

"Thank you, Madeline," said Lincoln. "First I want you all to know how excited I am about this project. Second, we must absolutely maintain radio silence about the project. Talk up the charity as much as you want, but nothing about SUNFLOWER. Loose lips sink ships. Last but not least, I need to tell you. We are only able to take one individual to Vegas for the meetings. That person will be my liaison for both the charity luncheon as well as the SUNFLOWER meeting."

Only one person could attend the meeting? She looked down at her notes and frowned. She had hoped since she was at the meeting that she would also be going to Vegas. But now? The chances of her going dropped down to next to nothing. Surely, the individual with the most seniority would go.

She frowned, but wasn't willing to give up entirely. There had to be a way to go with the team to Vegas. She had barrel raced in high school and knew the meaning of grit. There was always a way to win.

No way was she giving up. Somehow, she'd figure out how to make herself invaluable. Meeting the Donohoe family, August and Yukika would happen. Chloe made up her mind. She was going to Vegas. She was willing to do anything. Anything.

"We don't have it in our budget to include more of you at this point. Instead of me telling you who will go, I've decided that you must decide amongst yourselves." The Congressman nodded to Madeline. "Let me know as soon as possible who will be the appointed liaison."

"We'll do that sir. Any thoughts on how you want us to proceed?"

"May the best woman win. I've got to leave for a meeting, I trust you to take things from here." He gave Katherine a knowing look, then gathered his polished leather case and left the room.

The room was silent. Chloe glanced at Cheyenne, who then shrugged.

"Indeed," Madeline said, turning from the closed door to the women around the conference table. "Don't worry. We will figure something out."

Chapter 2

The Capital Hill Bar was a drinking establishment for the worker bees of the Hill. The walls were exposed brick. Industrial white lights hung from the ceiling. Popular music played quietly in the background. Loud enough to sing to, but low enough to hear conversation.

The back wall was a library of booze. Chloe glanced at the top shelf wondering what liquor was up there. How many people actually ordered alcohol from the top shelf? Was the wooden ladder leaning against the wall for show?

The happy hour crowd was vibrant. People seemed thrilled to be out of the office to meet up with friends and have a drink. Chloe was used to the college side of town, and didn't get over much to

Capitol Hill, so it was nice to be in a sea of fresh faces. Walking through the crowd, being a part of the daily life that made politics and thus history, Chloe felt happy with her job choice for the summer. She'd never be written about in actual history books, but she didn't care, she was a cog that helped turn the wheel.

In the middle of the bar was an island of stand-up cocktail tables. Opal had pushed two tables together so they'd have enough space for their group. Chloe, Cheyenne, and Opal, the assistants, arrived first. Eleanor showed up ten minutes later. When Madeline, Katherine, and Lizbeth walked in, Chloe swore the whole bar was quiet while everyone turned to look at the three power-players, but only for a moment, and soon enough the din returned.

"I'm so glad everyone could meet up tonight," said Katherine. "I was worried your schedules were all going to be busy tonight."

Katherine. Her new boss. She was petite and strawberry-blonde, but her personality was that of an Irish firebrand. Chloe was amazed that such a commanding presence came from such a little thing, and she had liked her immediately. She had an aunt like her, so was used to the strong disposition. She was the only woman in the group who wore something besides a block of dark color. She had on a light-colored black and white plaid skirt with hints of pink shading and a matching suit jacket.

They had met at the university book store. Earlier in the year, Chloe happened on an article in a school newsletter that the Congressman would be signing books later that afternoon at the university bookstore. She ran back to her dorm to find her worn copy of the Congressman's book and grabbed a copy of her resume already printed from a job fair. *You never know.*

At the lecture, Chloe asked the questions she had marked up in the back of the book when she first read it. Both the Congressman and his senior aide were intrigued and impressed with her line of thought. After the reading, Chloe approached Katherine with her resume. She glanced it over. Chloe studied her poker face, unable to tell whether she liked it or not. To her surprise, Katherine hired her on the spot. Said she liked her spunk. Without thinking, Chloe accepted.

"Well, we do need to celebrate Chloe's arrival," said Cheyenne lifting a wine glass up to her. Chloe lifted her wine glass with a smile to return the cheer. Cheyenne was her age and had bright summer blonde hair. She was tall, but not as tall as Madeline.

Madeline smiled at the comment, but had not yet looked up. She typed like a mad woman on her phone. She was Katherine's opposite: tall and lanky with dark brown hair. She wore her hair loose, but it seemed perfectly coiffed, even at the end of a long day. Her shoes were to die for, Chloe had seen the pair in the latest Barney's catalog. On her right wrist hung an expensive diamond and sapphire tennis bracelet.

Katherine glared at Madeline. "Of course we do ... Madeline? Madeline! Let's welcome Chloe." Katherine raised her glass to Chloe. The women clinked glasses together with words of cheers and a salud. Whatever happened, this would be a very interesting evening.

"Now that that's over, and not that you aren't important Chloe, but we need to figure out who is going to Vegas," continued Katherine.

Chloe was taken aback by the comment, but unfazed. When she first moved to DC, the direct-ness almost offended her, but she quickly learned the East Coast communication style. She was used to it now. She believed Katherine had no intention of belittling her, but rather, she was simply getting to the point.

"Why couldn't he just pick by seniority? This is

ridiculous," said Lizbeth. She straightened her suit jacket. "I mean, why this little game?"

"That would put you in first place with seniority then, right Lizbeth?" teased Katherine with a smile.

Lizbeth gave her a sharp glance back. "I have earned it."

Lizbeth was always so serious. Even the part in her hair was severe and perfect.

"Link is not playing any game," replied Eleanor. "He trusts us enough to come up with the best candidate. Madeline, what are you doing? Get off your phone. We need you!"

"I'm almost done. Hold on." But, she didn't take her eyes off her smart phone.

"I say we just pick straws then. We are all pretty much the same caliber, right?" asked Opal. The women at the table stared at her.

"Straws?" asked Lizbeth.

Chloe felt bad for her. Opal's cheeks flushed.

"It's just an idea."

"Opal is right," said Madeline, not bothering to look at Opal. "Send! Okay. Apologies, I'm with you now." She made eye contact and smiled at Opal. Chloe thought her smile was on the saccharine side, but who was she to judge? She had just met the woman.

"I have the perfect idea," said Madeline. "And, it'll be fun, too. We are all single, right? Chloe, do you have a significant other?"

Chloe looked up from her white wine. An image of her ex-boyfriend flashed through her mind. Chloe hadn't dated seriously since high school. She was a junior when her ex had moved to join the rodeo circuit. He was kind of a bad boy, and she adored him.

Jack rode a Ducati and broncos in the rodeo. He was a charmer, and he liked to live fast. They had sex a few times. While it was good, she never experienced anything cataclysmic. They broke up because neither of them were willing to pursue a long-distance relationship. Chloe had loved him, but she pragmatically believed a boyfriend was a waste of time. So was sex for that matter.

"No, I don't have a boyfriend. I'm in law school, what time do I have for a man?"

"Great. Okay. We are all single. With that, I propose that we play a BINGO game of sorts. First, you meet a man, perhaps like a lobbyist or a fundraiser, and then...you kiss him. The first girl to spell BINGO wins."

"Come on Madeline, very funny. Let's have a

random drawing like Opal suggested. I'll get the straws," said Eleanor.

"Oh no, ladies. We are going to have fun with this game. Vegas is high stakes. The individual who goes? This will change her career, change her life path even," she said, her gaze focused on Cheyenne and Chloe.

"So dramatic," said Lizbeth. "Don't be ridiculous. It's a meeting in Vegas. We don't need one of your crazy ideas."

Madeline narrowed her eyes as she looked at Liz. "Come on Liz. Don't downplay this. And besides, you always end up loving my crazy ideas."

Liz snorted in a way that she seemed moderately appalled and yet perhaps there might be a kernel of truth to her statement.

Madeline swished back her auburn hair. "It's true Liz and you know it. You always end up loving my ideas."

A courier walked into the Capital Hill Bar. Madeline raised her hand, waving him over. He handed her a manila envelope and she signed off on his electronic clipboard.

"Here are the BINGO cards I made up, just now. That's the beauty of having a Send To Printer app on my phone. Now. The point. The BINGO game is to kiss five different men at five different monuments."

"You're crazy," said Lizbeth. "We can't have a kiss and tell contest."

"Yes. We can. Here are the cards." Madeline handed out a card to each of the women. "Don't lose these, I've deleted the info already," she said directing the information towards Eleanor. "The kicker is that you have to kiss them at one of the monuments. The Jefferson Memorial, The Lincoln Memorial etc. This game will be quite exciting. I promise you."

"No way," said Opal. "Whoever works the hardest should go."

"Let's just stop being so selfish," said Madeline. "Chloe here is new to this side of town and what better way for her to have a chance at this trip? And also get to know the locals?"

"I'm in," said Cheyenne, flipping her wavy hair back. "It's sort of fun and flirty. God knows I need some of that."

"Are you kidding? A kissing game?" asked Eleanor. "I can't believe this."

"I am partial to the idea," said Katherine. "I don't know why though. It is crazy."

Madeline rolled her eyes and tipped her head

back for emphasis. "It's *just* a kiss, it's not sex. I'm not asking you to prostitute yourselves. It's just, you know, something ... different. Something fun."

Liz shook her head and crossed her arms. "If we get caught, the Congressman will have our asses."

"I never get caught," said Eleanor. It was as if Liz had thrown down a challenge and Eleanor rose to meet it. "I'm in."

"So far, that's me, Katherine, Cheyenne, and Eleanor. What about the rest of you?" asked Madeline.

Opal looked down at her Vodka tonic. A maraschino cherry floated on the top and she stirred her drink. She still had not yet responded and looked outside the window.

"We'll need proof though, of some sort," said Katherine. "A selfie on Instagram with an image of the monument. Fancy it up if you want."

"Tag each other. Make sure you're friends with everyone before the night is over," said Cheyenne. "Helps keep the game honest. Chloe, let's do it. It'll be a lot of fun, and honestly, a different way to meet guys."

"Okay. I'm in. But, I don't know, do I even have a chance?" Chloe replied, looking down at her

BINGO sheet. "I wouldn't know how to find a lobbyist or a fundraiser, or any of these people."

"Stick with me, I'll help you. Is this your Instagram?" Cheyenne held her smartphone up to Chloe, who nodded.

Was she going to play a freaking kissy-kissy BINGO game? Hell yes. Especially if it might mean it would be her only chance to get to Vegas. After this morning's meeting, she planned to do some maneuvering to get on the team to Vegas, but now all she had to do was win this BINGO game. Just kiss five guys first and win. That should be easy.

Madeline lifted up her BINGO card and a Cheshire grin appeared. "Check, check, and check!"

"Honestly? You guys, I'm way too busy for this," Liz said. "I've got a hundred Chinese people coming in on Thursday and the guy I was working with at State ended up on emergency family leave. I have no idea how well-prepped his replacement is and..." She paused, took a deep breath. "Look it doesn't matter. You guys go for it. As much as Vegas sounds like fun, I don't have time for these kinds of games." She tipped her wine glass towards Madeline and eyed the other women around the table. "You all should keep your eyes on Madeline. Even if I'm not playing I think every single letter must be earned from this day forward. No back-dated kisses."

"We are looking at you dear," said Kat, winking at Madeline. "En Garde!"

"And lose out on an opportunity to meet new men? Never!" Madeline's elbow swung back into a fencing defense pose. "I would never squander such an opportunity. If we are going to play this game, all of us have to play." Madeline said, honing in on Opal, "and all of us have to swear to secrecy."

"Oh alright. I'll play," replied Opal. Chloe didn't think she looked very enthusiastic. "And, of course, I'll swear to secrecy." Opal held up her pinky finger in the middle of the group. Madeline, Katherine, Lizbeth, Eleanor, Cheyenne, and Chloe all held up their glasses. Opal blushed and brought down her pinky before raising her glass.

"To secrecy!" said Madeline.

"To secrecy!" repeated the women in unison. They clinked and each took a sip. They seemed jubilant, but Chloe could have sworn they warily eyed the other.

OPAL HAD FINISHED her drink and was off to the

bathroom. She stopped mid-way and answered her phone. She glanced around quickly, then took off down the hall.

Sketchy. Chloe had only been at the office for a short time and already the girls had filled her in on Opal. Katherine said she was fantastic, that she could handle the menial to the mighty, but, as a result, everyone in the office dumped all their stuff on her. She always said *yes.* Cheyenne told her they actually nicknamed her 'The Dump.' That kind of nickname seemed really mean; it surprised Chloe.

She had read up on the personnel profiles from the Congressman's webpage. Opal was a Harvard graduate, she had interned for a prominent Wall Street office, and had spent a year in Eastern Europe with Peace Corps. On paper, Opal should be the rodeo queen of the office, but instead, she was the dumping ground. She wondered why for a brief moment, then glossed over the curiosity with a conclusion that she did not want to end up like Opal. Chloe planned to play BINGO, and she planned to win.

She swirled the drink in her hand and watched the wine legs come down the glass. In order to finish the BINGO game first, Chloe had to kiss five guys in the span of two weeks. What had she gotten herself into? Was this some sort of political casting couch? While she didn't like the idea of kissing that many guys in two weeks, going to Vegas with Lincoln Pierce would be worth every awkward and chaste kiss. If she won, she would meet Jack Donohue, August Thorne, and Yukika Matthews. Leaders in the industry. This meeting, without a doubt, would lead her to the Big Time, to the people who mattered in DC.

The Capital Bar and Lounge turned down the lights. By ten pm, Madeline, Liz, and Eleanor had called it a night and headed out. The first round of happy hour people had gone home, and new people arrived. The second wave she called it. There was still a large crowd and she scanned it to see if anyone in the immediate vicinity was remotely attractive to kiss.

The absurdity hit her. What was she just going to meet some random guy and kidnap him to one of the memorials? This was ridiculous. She heard a commotion and looked over. Opal had tripped on something and was picking herself up off the ground. The hell if she would end up like Opal.

She saw a guy in the crowd who looked relatively cute. Chloe didn't want to approach him, so she called over the waitress and asked her if she knew the cute guy across the room, thinking he might be a regular. The waitress didn't recognize him. Chloe asked her point blank if she should buy him a drink. The 'hell no' look on the waitress's face answered her question.

Opal came back to the table and hung her purse on a hook installed beneath the table. "You wouldn't believe what just happened to ..."

"I have something important to say," Cheyenne said. "And you too, Opal. If you leave with someone, I want to make sure you're safe. If you can't tell me that you're leaving, then text me a picture of the guy's business card or something, okay?"

"Good idea." Chloe liked that Cheyenne was looking out for her, for all of them really. She quickly glanced at Opal, to make sure she was alright. She seemed a little put off, but well, there was a man in play and she didn't have time to ask her if she was okay. She glanced back to the man who caught her attention. All she wanted to know was his job title. "Cheyenne, go ask that guy for his business card."

"No I won't. Do your own dirty work," said Cheyenne, regarding her empty glass. "I am going to the bar to order another round of drinks. I'll be back."

Chloe looked over at Opal. Maybe Opal would

do it, maybe she could get Opal to ask the guys out for her. *That's it! I'll have Opal do all the meet and greet parts. Then I can decide whether or not the guy is worthy.* Chloe knew she couldn't outright ask her, so she started with an opener.

"Opal, what were you about to say earlier?"

"I got this call," she said, "and it was from..."

Cheyenne was back. She gave Opal a dirty look, interrupting her. "The waitress caught me on the way to the bar. She's going to get our drinks and bring them back."

Opal stopped talking and stammered, "I...I...I have to go to the bathroom. I'll be right back."

What the hell?

"Don't you dare get Opal to meet guys for you either. You get out there, honey. Do you need someone to show you how? You can watch me and learn." Cheyenne picked up her drink. She went up to the cute guy Chloe had been scoping out and in less than eight seconds, she got his business card. She faced Chloe and waved it at her with a smirk on her face. *Damn. That girl did not mess around.*

But for this BINGO game? If she wanted to win, she'd have to buck up. If not, she would lose for sure. She set down her wine glass and ordered an ice water.

"I heard you were looking to buy a drink for someone," asked a deep voice. His accent was definitely not DC, but bourbon smooth Southern. She turned, expecting him to be eye to eye, but instead found herself looking at a very expensive tie striped with deep purple and fine lines of white. Chloe raised her eyes to meet a pair of deep brown eyes with black flecks, dark as night. "Don't buy that guy a drink," he said, he glanced over at Cheyenne and the cute guy. "Buy me one."

He must have heard her ask. She inhaled his scent of cedarwood and patchouli. Chloe swallowed hard. A musky, masculine scent filled her nose, it was a scent that could not be denied. She held back from an instinctive urge to pull him into her, to pull the desirous smell close to her.

"Are you eavesdropping on me?" she asked, hand on her hip.

"A southern gentleman never tells." A smile, full of mischief, crossed over his face, but he kept his voice serious.

"Shouldn't a southern gentleman be buying a lady her drink?" *Two can play this game.*

"We live in modern times, darlin'," he said. "Name's Harrison."

A hint of black pepper mixed in with his smell. Her mouth started to water.

"I do know how to treat a woman, that much I can promise you."

His whole demeanor promised more than just manners. *And, what was under that shirt? Something good.* Chloe's center was hot and she felt her face turn red. *Get ahold of yourself.* She took a drink of wine.

"Are you blushing already darlin'?"

"Did you just darlin' me?"

The amber-flecks in his brown eyes condensed into a darker shade, if that was possible, daring her to take him on. He smiled again. *And his lips.* His lips were indeed full and oh so very kissable. Would he taste spicy hot or would he be sweet, like a beignet?

"I did. I'm from NOLA," he said. "But, saying NOLA leaves something to be desired, too newfangled for me. New Orleans. There. That sounds better."

She loved the way his tongue rolled over the r in Orleans. The way he said it felt like the unrolling of a red carpet. Welcoming. Exciting. She moistened her lips. "I've never been down that way. You wrassle with alligators?" She asked with a fake accent. She twirled a hair that had gotten loose from her bun and jutted up her chin.

"At least you didn't ask about Mardi Gras," he said. His gaze intensified, as if he was about to tangle with her and toss down. Her body reacted naturally. Her breath quickened and she felt her nipples harden against the soft bra.

"I've always wanted to ride one of those boats with the giant fan, but they don't look very safe," she said with a devilish smile. For some reason, she said it coquettishly, as if she were a belle at the ball.

"You'd be safe with me." He stood up tall and squared his shoulders.

Collecting herself with a drink of ice water rather than wine, she asked, "What brings you all the way to DC?"

The features in his face became tender and tough at the same time. Whatever it was he did for a living, he loved it for sentimental reasons, and she knew he'd defend it from hell to high water.

"All of us are lawyers, right? Darlin', what are you drinking?"

Strange. He didn't answer the question. Usually when she had asked someone what they did, a five-minute explanation ensued. Modest perhaps? She wasn't sure, but really, it was of no consequence to her. Lawyer was one of the options on the BINGO sheet, at the Jefferson Memorial if her memory served her right. *Perfect!* Without question, she would enjoy kissing him and she'd have a B crossed off. She looked back up at him with a devious gleam.

"I don't know what you are thinking," he said, brushing something imaginary off her shoulder. "But, I have a feeling that I will like it immensely."

The sexy drawl made her core go from hot to blazing. He was a BINGO kiss. Her plan formed in half a second. They would take a cab to the Jefferson Memorial. Then she would kiss him. Take a cab home. Wake up alone. Go to work like usual. She preferred to leave him after the kiss. That would be the sensible choice with work being busy and needing to win BINGO by kissing four more men. But if she was going to play this BINGO game, she had to act quickly before her nerves got the better of her.

"Come with me," she said. Her heart pounded with the buzz that reminded her of the rodeo signal to start. *Game on.* She leaned in close to him, the smell of him making her woozy, and whispered, "You and I are going on a secret mission."

His face lit up. He reached out and took her elbow, then slid his hand, firm but gentle, down to her wrist then tapered off. His slight touch made all thoughts cloudy. She was actually wet. His touch, that was all it took. and she could feel the dampness in her panties. Well … maybe she'd do more than kiss him.

"Now, now, Caiman. A secret mission? Hmm. I like a lady to take charge. Every once in a while."

"So? Are you coming or not?" she asked, not knowing or caring about the meaning of caiman, but instead wanting to engage him.

He cracked his knuckles. "A secret mission or you just taking advantage of a country boy?"

"Country boy my ass." She took his hand. His rough skin surprised her. Chloe walked him through the bar. At the door, she tried to catch Cheyenne's eye to let her know she was going. Cheyenne happened to look up and Chloe held out her hand and called out, "I'll text you later!" Her friend waved goodbye. At least she would be one up on Opal.

On the sidewalk, she planned to let go of his hand, but his grip tightened around hers. Even under his shirt, she saw his fantastic biceps. With her free hand, she hailed a cab. A car pulled up, she dropped his hand and held his chest back.

"Taking charge again. Where to, Caiman?" he asked, a mischievous smile playing on his lips. He scratched the side of his cheek. The five o'clock shadow made him look rugged around his polished edges. One look at his handsome face and his muscled body, Chloe wasn't sure if she could stop, she wasn't sure of anything.

"You'll find out soon enough," she said.

CHLOE LEANED INTO THE CAB, one knee was on the seat, the other on the sidewalk, and her ass up in the air. She spoke to the driver in hushed tones so Harrison wouldn't hear, but she was pretty certain Harrison was focused on her, at least on her derriere. He wouldn't hear a thing.

She parted her thighs and lifted her cheeks--just a smidgen--against the fabric of her skirt. Cool air rushed against her wet clit. Her body tensed, and savored the unexpected pleasure. She sat down in the cab and patted the seat next to her. Harrison got into the cab. He adjusted his tie, loosening it up. His eyes were hooded with desire. He swallowed and she watched his Adam's apple bob.

"Where are we going?" he asked and slid his hand under her knee.

"That's part of the secret." This was the first

time she had ever done anything like this. She was always the responsible one. The bravery emboldened her.

"Aren't you a sassy one? I'll play along with your little game, Caiman." He hadn't taken his eyes off her yet.

Even though she wanted to sit closer to him, to feel his skin against her own, she decided to keep a little distance. She didn't want to get too close, she just wanted a kiss.

Chapter 3

Chloe blurted out, "It is your lucky day Harrison." She felt silly saying this, but tried not let it show in her face. She'd never tried to get a guy to kiss her before, it was always the other way around. Adrenaline raced through her blood vessels. She took a deep breath to calm herself down. She had no idea what to say, so she said the first thing that came to mind. "You get to be the one who helps me fulfill a bucket list."

Chloe slipped her hand inside her shirt to pull up a fallen bra strap. Harrison's eyes followed her every move, darkening again when her hand slipped beneath her shirt.

"And what exactly is on your bucket list?"

"I've always wanted to kiss someone at one of

the monuments. It's kind of sexy." She had meant to wait until they got to the monument to explain herself, but she couldn't hold herself back.

"Un p'tit bec? That's Cajun for kiss. What makes you think I want only one kiss?" He moved his hand from below her knee to on top of her thigh. With his fingertips, he firmly but lightly traced it towards her hip, burning a path of fire on her thigh.

Her mouth salivated, she swallowed heavily. "It'll be fun."

"Sure you can stop at one kiss?" His fingertips reached towards her inner thigh and he pressed down.

She gave him a smile: half temptress, half innocent.

"Of course only one kiss. What kind of girl do you take me for?"

"One who needs to be kissed properly."

Chloe shh'd him, then glanced in the direction of the cab driver. His attention was on the road though, not on the occupants in the back seat.

"Why don't you sit closer, Caiman? Afraid you'll bite?"

Before Chloe could respond, the cab pulled up to the monument and stopped the meter.

"Twelve fifty please."

Chloe moved to get the money out of her purse, but Harrison was faster and handed the driver a twenty.

"You didn't have to do that."

"Yes I did. My momma raised me right."

The saying made her smile. Cliché as it was, it did not sound trite when a hot guy from New Orleans said it with a sexy Southern accent.

One kiss. No more than that. Sex wasn't all that exciting anyways. It was usually a letdown after all the intense flirting. One moment she was turned on hotter than a fry at the carnival, next thing you know, she was colder than an icy pop.

Besides, she needed to focus on work for the next few months. She didn't have time for a fling, an affair, or a boyfriend, or a, well, whatever this was. She needed to win the BINGO game. She wouldn't win if she got attached to every single guy she kissed.

One kiss. Sweet. Harmless. Most importantly, singular.

Harrison held his hand out for her. Chloe took it, and he pulled her out of the vehicle. The palms of his hand had a few callus's and she wondered what work he did with them. Woodwork? Maybe they were from sports. What she wanted to know was how his hands would feel as he touched her body.

She blushed at the thought and quickly glanced at him. He was a babe. Taller than her at 6'5". He was a well-muscled man with wavy black hair. He was well dressed in an expensive navy suit and wore Ferragamo shoes. And his lips? They were totally made to kiss--with a sweet little cupid bow on his upper lip.

Stop it! He is just a kiss.

Did she have to stop though? Her whole life, she had always been the one to make responsible choices. When her friends got too drunk at the bar, she drove them home. Maybe she didn't have to be so sensible this time.

Tonight is not about prudence. Tonight is about winning.

With that thought in mind, she took her cell from her purse, and checked into the Jefferson Memorial on Instagram, tagging Cheyenne and Madeline. She wrote 'To B or not to B' thinking herself clever.

They walked around to the front of the memorial and stopped to admire the tidal basin. During the day, tourists pedaled white boats around and snapped pictures of the Japanese cherry blossoms, when they were in season. The smell of spring turning summer drifted to her nose. A few trees were still in bloom late May. He enfolded her hand into his. She lifted her chin to him. He brushed the hair back from her face.

Under the sea... No. NO. Stop. She would control herself.

"Follow me." He led her up the steps and into the white marbled memorial to the inner sanctum. Chloe had imagined herself taking the reins, but was enthused by his response. They walked through the memorial and to a place behind the statue and in the columns. The temperature dropped a few degrees under cover and the smell of marble dust grew stronger. His spicy smell mixed in with the cooling humidity and late blooming flowers. The night air was heavy and sultry, and she relished the perfumed cherry blossom scent. He put his arm around her waist and guided her towards him.

"Just one kiss?" His breath was hot against her neck.

Chloe found herself unable to answer him with words, "Mmm hmm." All she wanted was his lips on hers, to find out if he tasted sweet or spicy. The spring night breeze tousled his hair.

"One kiss then." He pulled her into his arms, pulled her tight. With his free hand, he cupped the back of her head and brought her in for a kiss. His tongue opened her lips and explored her mouth.

She gasped. He tasted salty and sweet. Chloe's jaw went slack and she met his tongue. They darted in and out of each other's mouth, tasting and teasing. He bit her lip, then his sweet lips moved down her neck, tiny kisses dotting her neck. He moved back up, and scratched the side of her cheek with stubble from his own cheek. Her knees went a little weak. Desire exploded through her. She took in the bottom of his ear lobe with her mouth, sucked it, and then gave him a soft nibble.

Harrison pulled back with a sweet grin. "You do bite, Caiman."

Chloe giggled. "What does caiman mean, anyway?"

"It's a wild thing of the deep, an alligator." Harrison pressed her waist closer to his hips where she felt a heat rising.

Chloe rested her hands on his lower back and pressed them up following his natural V shape. A low, animalistic growl escaped his lips. He came back to her mouth, kissing her deeply. His hand came up under her shirt. He pulled back the bra to take her nipple between his knuckles. Chloe groaned with pleasure, and Harrison stopped. He was looking down at her with a wicked grin.

"One kiss, Caiman."

Chloe was breathless and panting. She swallowed. "One kiss?"

"One kiss," he said, stepping back to arm's length.

The distance between them was suddenly a chasm, the cool night air fluttering between them. She wanted to jump across and back into his arms. "Technically you already gave me two."

"You got lucky tonight darlin'." He took her hand and lead her to the cab drop off. "The truth is sweetheart, I want to wait for you." He rubbed his fingers against her palm.

What did he mean by that?

She didn't know what to say to him. Harrison flagged down a cab that had just dropped off another couple. She had hoped for more time with him. Before she got in, he stepped in close. His smell assaulted her senses. She wanted to kiss him again. No, she had to be honest with herself. She wanted more than just a kiss.

He brushed the loose hairs away from her face, and leaned in to whisper in her ear. "Until next time. Au revoir, Caiman."

Chloe was unsure how she got into the cab, how she separated from his body, but she was a quivering mess all the way home. At her apartment in Dupont Circle, she tried to pay for the cab, but Harrison had already prepaid the driver.

She went into her bedroom and immediately took her clothes off. They were too hot and restrictive. She opened a window to let air in, but it was hot and sticky. She switched the fan on.

Restless energy coursed through her. How could she possibly get to sleep when all she could think about was Harrison? She wanted to breathe in his heady scent. She wanted to surrender to his sweet lips. She wanted to feel his rough yet gentle hands on her naked skin.

One kiss indeed. She flopped onto her bed, pulled the covers up and kicked them off again. She grabbed her extra pillow and wrapped her lonely arms around it, then tossed it away. She tried her back. Her stomach. Her side. Her mind raced, and her body hummed with unsated need.

She didn't masturbate all that often. While it felt pretty good, she could never bring herself to a rising height that made it worthwhile. Tonight would be different though. Tonight she had Harrison's sweet voice in her head, his "Au Revoir, Caiman" a sweet serenade.

She instinctively ran her hands over her body, pretending they were his. She slipped a pillow under her hips. She played with her nipples. They were still rock hard from his touch, she pinched one while the other hand slipped down between her legs. Her finger slowly circled her clit, swollen with need.

With Harrison on her mind, her body responded quickly. She rubbed back and forth until a rhythm kicked in, and soon, waves of an orgasm pummeled through her. She cried out and bit her lip, letting the storm rumble through her body.

If it was this amazing on my own, how incredible would it be with him?

Exhausted, she sprawled out on her bed. She was unsure if she wanted to put pajamas on or take a shower.

You'll never see him again, so who cares?

Definitely, she needed a cold shower.

Chapter 4

Chloe drifted in and out of a light sleep. Around five a.m., she got up and took another cold shower. She dressed in a black skirt, a crisp, white button down, and a nice hand painted silk scarf in swirling colors of yellow and white. She hopped the Metro to work. While on the train, she organized her thoughts. She planned to tell the girls that she got her first stamp on the BINGO card. Her proof was a check in on Instagram.

On the train, Chloe crossed her ankles. What would she tell the girls about the kiss itself? They would ask. She tugged her bottom lip. The memory of his kiss and his taste warmed her body, the subtle movements of the Metro a reminder of what she wanted. No. She didn't dare tell anyone how she felt about the kiss. He was just a kiss, a nice sweet inno-cent little kiss. That's all anyone needed to know.

She needed four more if she was going to be the one going to Vegas, where she would get to meet August Thorne and Yukika Matthews. The two biggest entrepreneurs in the country. To have a chance like this and miss out because she was smitten over a kiss?

Hell no. Buck up buttercup. Forget about Harrison.

In the office, she poured coffee into her favorite silver to-go mug. It kept the coffee hotter and longer than a ceramic mug, and she could sling it from meeting to meeting. She added Irish creamer, and pretended it was an homage to her ancestors. At her desk, she organized her day and started to answer emails.

A few minutes later, Madeline entered the office. Her long coat swished in along with her hair and her purse. She seemed rushed, but Chloe couldn't figure out why, she was right on time. Her eyes seemed a little bloodshot though. As if on cue, Madeline pulled out a bottle of Visine and added a few drops to each eye.

"I hate being hung over," she said bluntly taking a sip of her grande Starbucks. Looking over to Chloe, she seemed to assess her. "I saw you checked in at the Jefferson."

"Yeah. New Orleans hottie. Lawyer. We kissed," she said brazenly. She hoped her clipped sentence would mask the desire she felt to kiss Harrison again.

"You look a little doe-eyed there, sweet farm girl. You in love already?"

"No. Me? That's crazy. I just, it was just one kiss. No big deal."

"Are you sure?" Madeline studied her face.

"Did you see they put new creamers by the coffee? They have Irish Crème and Hazelnut flavors. They're good."

"I can't drink that stuff," she said, offering no reason why. "Stop trying to change the subject. Will you see him again?"

"No. I sent him home in a cab like a good girl," she said, telling a little white lie. She remembered his last words, his rough skin against the side of her face as he whispered them to her, and her heat thrummed against her ribs. To combat her desire, she quickly added, "I didn't bother to get his information since I'll be winning this little contest and headed to Vegas."

"Hmmph. We'll see about that," responded Madeline tartly. "And, you're blushing. You really do like this guy." At her desk, she pulled up a two-tone vintage leather briefcase and opened it, retrieving several manila folders bound together by a rubber band. "Katherine wanted me to give you this packet. She isn't able to make a meeting this morning with one of the lawyers. Check your email for specifics of where and when."

"Will do." Chloe wanted to ask if Katherine was too hungover to attend the meeting, but thought better of it and kept quiet.

Congressman Pierce came into the office. He was dressed in a pinstripe suit with a power red tie. Even though he was extremely busy, he almost always said good morning to her or at least nodded in her direction. This time, he stopped at her desk.

"Good morning. Is the constituent list ready?" he asked. Part of her job was to collate all the constituent emails and snail mail into one spreadsheet containing the name, reason for writing, and the age, if pertinent. Lincoln Ulysses Pierce was a man of the people. He genuinely liked to keep in touch with his residents, but due to sheer volume had to prioritize which ones he could personally respond to.

Chloe had just finished the list and handed it to him. She thanked her lucky stars she had come in early. "If you want, in the future, I can leave it in your in box or email it to you."

"Email it to me please. Thank you, Chloe. Madeline, you ladies close to figuring out who will accompany me to Vegas?"

"No sir. Not yet. We're working on it."

"Great. Let me know as soon as you do." He strode off into his office closing the door behind him.

Chloe liked working for Lincoln. He didn't have the sleaze ball politician personality. Many politicians on the Hill came off like used car salesmen. So far from what she had seen in the office, he was genuine, and he cared about the people from his state. It didn't mean he was a softie, his arguments were a precise pitch of logic and emotion. His negotiations with other members of the Hill were legendary. A Capitol Hill internship, even if accidental, would be a notch in her belt.

Chloe took the packet Madeline had given her and started to look through the contents. The material consisted of the first draft proposals and draft legislation. There were environmental impact assessments, financial data, and Return On Investment calculations that detailed both environmental and economic benefits.

She logged onto her email app and found

Katherine's email. She was to meet with the environmental lawyer to discuss the draft and talk next steps. The meeting would take place at 10:30 a.m. in a reserved conference room. The name of the environmental lawyer she'd be meeting with was Harrison Rousseau.

Everything went quiet, but her body felt electrified. She would have sworn she looked like a cartoon character with her eyes bulging out of her head.

No way. It couldn't be him.

She tried to convince herself that Harrison was a common name. A loud bang in the room startled her. Chloe looked towards the noise and made eye contact with Opal. She pushed up her glasses on her head and looked about to cry. Around her was a pile of papers she just dropped and they were scattered everywhere. Chloe stood up and walked over to her.

"Let me help you." While Chloe helped Opal pick up papers, she realized again that she wanted to be nothing like her. She especially did not want anyone to ever call her the Dump, even affectionately. She had to win this game. Opal thanked her profusely before she left the office on her way to a meeting.

"Even if it is Harrison," said Chloe to herself. "It

doesn't matter. I need to get four more kisses from four more men."

CHLOE STOPPED in the bathroom to freshen up. If it was Harrison, and she was sure it wouldn't be, then she should look nice and not frazzled. Chloe smoothed her hair and placed it behind her ears. It was the same movement he did right before putting her in the cab.

She felt a little unsteady. *Not now.* She tucked her shirt in so it was even and adjusted the thin belt. *Better.* Finally, she puckered up her lips and added matte lipstick. With a determined breath, she glanced over the image in the mirror and smiled.

Carry on dear.

Her high heels clipped with purpose down the hallway. She had her to-go silver coffee cup and the stack of papers, along with her laptop. She passed by historical works of art involving the nation's history: civil war, revolutionary war, portraits, and pastoral scenes.

She loved working in this building, the dusty smell of marble, the constant echo of footsteps. Soon, by attending the Vegas conference, she'd be party to an historical event. She could parlay the event as a springboard for her career. With luck, she'd be here every day, working her way up to be someone like Katherine, or even Liz.

When she saw Harrison standing there, checking his phone, she almost dropped her coffee. He had spotted her. His gaze was intense, undressing her with his eyes. His walk confident, his stride powerful and headed straight for her. Last night, she had thought she was in control, but his walk clearly stated Alpha Male. With plans. Plans that involved her.

"I told you we'd see each other again," he said with his signature husky voice.

"How did you? What are you talking about?" she stammered.

"I saw Katherine last night at the bar. Just before she left, she told me that she wouldn't make the meeting today. She pointed you out."

"And when were you planning on telling me?"

"I was going to tell you, but I thought it'd be more fun to follow your lead."

Chloe let out an exasperated gasp.

"This way my dear," he said. She tried to walk confidently next to him, to keep her body from touching him. What she really wanted was for him to take her into the conference room for some privacy, push her up against the wall, and hike her skirt up. Or pinch her nipple. Or kiss her like no tomorrow. She needed him to touch her.

"Oh for shitcans on a peabed." She said under her breath, trying to divert herself. What she needed was to stop thinking about him.

He grinned back. "Now, now, Chloe. Don't you get your jaw worked up." Harrison leaned in, close enough to be private, but with enough distance to be somewhat professional. "Does my little caiman still bite?"

Shocked, she stammered, and took a step back. Swiftly, his hand was on her back, holding her steady.

"Easy there darlin'." He stabilized her with steady arms, then looked into her eyes. They were just like she remembered. Bottomless brown, café au lait, warm earth you could sink in, with flecks of black. He brought Chloe in, only an inch or so, but she was close enough to notice he was clean shaven this morning. Close enough to see the nick on his chin.

Gathering her senses, she said, "I'm okay. Let's get to the conference room."

He raised his eyebrows at her, as if double

checking that she'd be okay when he let go. She nodded. He stepped back and she regained her balance. *Barely.* They headed towards the conference room. Next to him, she felt the hairs on her arm raise towards him. Ugh! Even her damn hairs wanted to be near him.

Simmer down sister. Eyes on the BINGO prize.

She had to put thoughts of him away, especially if they were going to work together. Especially if she planned on going to Vegas.

Walking towards them was a red-headed man with his hair lightly gelled in a Caesar's cut. He wore a gray suit which accented his emerald green eyes and darkened his reddish hair.

He is good looking. Maybe he could be the next BINGO kiss. She forced herself to not think about Harrison. Forced herself to move on.

"Harrison!" he said, stopping to talk. Her eyes widened at him. Of course, he knows Harrison. She couldn't kiss the red head now.

"Gordy!" Replied Harrison with the same tone, "what brings you to this part of town?"

"Important meetings. Important people. You know. And who is this? I don't believe I've had the pleasure," he said. His smile was meant to convey amiable curiosity, but his gaze had the impact of being dangerous, raising the hairs on the back of her neck.

He reminded her of Jack, her ex. Even though the attraction between them was palpable, she instinctively knew she'd have to be careful around this one.

"Gordy meet Chloe. I have a meeting with her. She works for Congressman Pierce."

"Pleasure to meet you," he said and stuck out his hand towards her. She shook it back. "Why are you meeting with Harrison?" he asked, holding onto her hand.

"Easy there Gordon. Hands off. We're not secretly meeting. If that were the case, we'd be off site."

"Just making sure the oil and gas man is present if he needs to be." Gordy lifted her hand and gently kissed the back, his eyes twinkling a brilliant green.

Chloe's mouth slightly dropped and her eyes went wide.

"Oh, I apologize about the kiss," he said gently letting go of her hand. "My Southern manners just took over."

"If this was important, I'd be meeting with Katherine," Harrison said. He unbuttoned his suit jacket and squared his shoulders. "Chloe's just an intern. For fuck's sake Gordy, try using your brain. You want to be senior lobbyist someday, right?"

Just an intern?

She glared at Harrison. Who the hell did Harrison think he was, introducing her as some lowly intern? True, she was just an intern, but he didn't have to say it with such contempt in his voice.

Gordy winked at her. She smiled back; she kind of liked him.

Where was lobbyist on her Bingo Card? She thought maybe it was at the Washington Monument.

"Harrison. You're funny. Good thing we went to grad school together, or I'd be all over your shit."

"Bullshit. That never stopped you."

"Where did you go wrong, man? You should be one of us."

"Have to go. We do have a meeting." He glanced down at Chloe protectively.

She narrowed her eyes at him, still seething over the intern comment. Maybe moving on to kiss number two wouldn't be so hard after all.

"Alright alright, be on your way. See you at the game then?"

"Can't make it this week. Work. Let's go," he said sharply to Chloe, ushering her down the hall.

ONCE THEY WERE in the conference room and the door shut, Chloe let him have it.

"Get your hands off me." She turned on him and mimicked in a sing-songy voice, "she's just an intern."

"You are. Is that fact going to be awkward or difficult for you?" he asked, placing his hands on the back of a chair and leaning into her. He was obviously used to conflict and handled it with ease.

More than anything though, she wanted to ruffle his smooth good ol' boy feathers. He infuriated her.

"I can do my job. Can you do yours?"

"Caiman. Easy now. Don't bite."

"Don't patronize me."

He stood back and gave her space. "Patronize you? Do you know who that was?"

"Apparently, his name is Gordy," she said. He still looked rather amused at her antics. "And something about oil and gas."

"At least you're listenin'. But you're not figurin' it out yet."

She stopped for a moment to consider his words and closed her eyes. If he was oil and gas why would he be important and why would Harrison introduce her as an intern with such disdain. It only took half a minute for her to deduce the reasons. Gordy would tank SUNFLOWER. As soon as she had the answer, she opened her eyes.

"That's my girl. Tell me."

"He's a lobbyist, probably against any kind of renewable. If he got an inkling that something was going down, that would not be good."

"Well done Caiman. You are quick. Alligators often are." His eyes twinkled and added with a serious tone,"but, until you know people or the players in town, best to keep your mouth shut and keep your ego in check. No offense."

"None taken." Even though she understood why he did it, she smarted over being called an intern, especially in the tone he used.

"Gordy will tank this deal faster than a card shark on a shady street."

"You got some sayings there, don't you?" Anger still laced her words. She didn't want to melt in his arms anymore, she wanted to give him a rude awakening.

"I just met you, Caiman. I hope we can work together. I'd hate it if we couldn't." Harrison said it as if it were a question. He approached and took her hand.

Chloe's mouth felt dry.

He squeezed her hand gently, waiting for her response. Even though she felt hot, even though there was slight throbbing in her core, she didn't stammer this time. She wasn't going to fall for him.

"I agree wholeheartedly," she said, confidently returning his gaze. "Katherine will want this document ready by this afternoon, if we're going to meet the two-week deadline."

He winked at her. "Nicely done, Caiman." She swore there was desire in his eyes.

"Let's get started."

He dropped her hand.

It suddenly felt cold. Jerk. *Just an intern.* Ugh. If he's not interested, that'll make it easier to play BINGO. She went to the opposite side of the room and sat down across from him. She willed herself to stay present, but it was hard not to get lost in his brown eyes. Chloe crossed her legs as tight as she could to quell the distracting throbbing and focused on the work.

The meeting went quickly. He was adept at discussing the details without losing the big picture. She was impressed with his vocabulary skills, and was only sidetracked once by his Adam's apple, bobbing up and down in some natural pattern.

After the meeting, they discussed next steps. He gave her his email and said to send over the notes when she finished. He didn't mention a thing about seeing her outside of work. Not even for coffee.

She could have sworn Harrison was toying with her, that he delighted in her tension. *It didn't matter.* One kiss was for the better, even if her body craved more. She had a game to play.

Chapter 5

Chloe was not a fan of meetings. She glanced around the room at all her coworkers. This 'team player' mentality was new to her. Sure, she worked and played well with others, but her whole life, she had always chosen sports comprised of individual merit like running or chess. She didn't play basketball. They didn't have soccer or volleyball at her school, there wasn't any money for sports programs and not enough kids anyway. She had barrel-raced horses at the rodeo, that might be considered a team sport.

Eleanor had marked up the white board with all sorts of her rules. It was moments like this when she liked to close her eyes and reminisce about being in the barn or riding her horse along the dusty trails at sunset.

When she opened her eyes, all she saw was Eleanor, droning on and on about protocol. She took a sip of her coffee. At least she had found a place that made great coffee, a little shop on the corner of her block. That made it marginally better.

"Now, when we get to Vegas, we are going to make sure certain protocols are set up to make sure we have clean communications."

Whatever happens in Vegas stays in Vegas.

She'd never been there before and wondered if it was true, did they ever turn the lights off? *Hmm. Who knows.* All she wanted was be a part of the meeting with Yukika and August.

"Lizbeth isn't able to make it today. She's totally focused on the Chinese gig," Katherine said. She opened up an 8x11 cardboard box filled with stapled papers. "I have a hard copy of the beta legislation we will draft up. I created this doc on my laptop on airplane mode and saved it to this thumb drive. I swear to God; the lobbyists always find out what we're doing. I've even wondered if they use hackers to lurk. So we're using this process to be safe."

Madeline scoffed. Chloe nodded in agreement with Katherine, thinking about Gordy.

"Some of you think it may be overkill, but we'd rather this stay off the net until we are ready to act. This legislation is too important," she said to the team. Looking down at Madeline, she pointedly added, "It is overkill, but you've seen what can happen. Let's give this bill a chance. There's always a compromise in the language of a bill when the parties have had open discussions versus economically motivated third parties."

Chloe took a sip of her coffee. *Keep it off the internet. Check.* Her mind wandered back to Vegas. Naturally, the casinos didn't turn the lights off, why would they? Money rolls twenty-four seven. And logically, if any industry should be interested in environmentally friendly practices, it should be them, to save some damn money on the electric bill.

"Thank you Chloe. Your work with Harrison gave us a fantastic start to this document. I'll be meeting with him this afternoon to advance our work." She smiled at Chloe.

Chloe beamed, her ears perked, and her demeanor brightened even if she didn't want to hear Harrison's name. "Katherine, is there anything I can do to help? You want me to come to the next meeting?"

She instantly regretted the offer to help. What if

she said yes and had to see Harrison again. That would be weird, especially with Katherine there.

"No. We've got to keep the office running, so stay on task, back at the office."

Chloe nodded professionally and tried to hide her disappointment. What was going on with her? One minute she was freaking out and the next she was upset that she couldn't see him.

The intense feeling of his kiss last night flooded her senses. She touched her bottom lip, remembering the way he pulled her body into his, the enveloping warmth of him. Obviously, she wanted to see him again no matter how many times she tried to convince herself that it wasn't a good idea.

"You and Harrison will be working together on the final documentation though, point by point, to find any issues, stress test it for loopholes, that sort of thing. Usually we don't have time, but, well, we'll see." Katherine checked off an item on her notepad.

Chloe felt as if she'd just jumped into an icy river. She only hoped her face remained impassive, she didn't want anyone to see how she felt and quickly glanced around the room. No one seemed to be paying attention to her.

"Eleanor. I'll need you to verify all incoming data and also work on precedence. If you find any new sources or ideas, feel free to pass that information along."

Katherine seemed awfully terse with Eleanor. Chloe wondered why. Had something happened between the two women? Or was she seeing tension that wasn't really there? Chloe assumed it had nothing to do with liking or disliking, but rather it was her Eastern European countenance. Eleanor was not a happy, smiley person; she was serious. Of all the staffers, Eleanor and Liz were most similar, even though they clearly had no relation.

"Madeline, your job is to keep this off the eyes and ears of the Hill until we're ready for the public. Eleanor can help you with the protocols. She used to work in private security. Let's not tank this before it's live."

"To, ah, misdirect the information, we may put up documentation on the server." Eleanor said glancing towards Katherine.

Chloe sensed some weird power-play going on between the two women, but it was very subtle.

"It's a good idea," Katherine said.

"Don't you worry ladies. This bill will look amazing. Once we're ready, we'll have no problem selling this in D.C. and to the public," said Madeline.

"There was someone I met yesterday who could ..." said Chloe, the lobbyist mention reminded her of Gordy. She ought to tell the team.

Madeline cut her off and refused to make eye contact with Chloe. "Let's talk about what matters. The important question is who will be attending the conference in Vegas."

Did she not hear her speaking or did she cut her off on purpose? Chloe couldn't tell. Was this how Opal felt? Frankly, at this early morning hour, she didn't care. Her feelings didn't get hurt that easily, but she was wary of Madeline now. The team needed to know about Gordy and to be on the lookout for the lobbyist, so she'd tell Katherine after the meeting instead of Madeline.

"Oh my God," said Opal under her breath. "This game, ugh."

Chloe noticed the whole room was quiet. Eleanor didn't seem all that excited about the game either.

"I've got three of the letters already," said Madeline. "B, N, and G."

"It's only Wednesday," said Chloe.

"Past guys do not count. It has to be a new guy and a new kiss," said Katherine.

"They are new guys. Every single one of them. If

I could have counted all my previous dates, I would have won already. But well, that wouldn't be fair to everyone."

Chloe must have been looking at her in shock because Madeline winked at her with a sly smile. "Obviously, I know the rules. I'm just very good at what I do. There you have it ladies. If you want to go to Vegas, you'll have to step up your game. I've been tracking and so far: Chloe has one letter. Cheyenne has two, and I have the most so far with three. On to the next meeting," said Madeline as she put her laptop into her leather bag.

Chloe felt jealous of Cheyenne and, well, practically everyone in the room. They all had a better chance of winning than she did. When was she going to find time to actually locate all these men? D.C. had a population of six million. Finding a lobbyist, a fundraiser, a foreign dignitary, and a CIA person sounded super easy, but so far it had been all but impossible for her. Guess she should have gone back to the bar by herself and tracked down another BINGO participant.

"What's got you so down?" asked Cheyenne, under her breath.

"Nothing. Just thinking about how I'm going to get to Vegas."

"Aren't we all?" said Cheyenne. "I'm having fun though. There are some hot guys in D.C. you know." She checked her watch. "Anyway, I've got to run. Another meeting." Cheyenne gathered her laptop. "Don't worry Chloe. I'll help you out, but for Pete's sake, don't be prissy like last time."

"What do you mean?"

Cheyenne looked up from her phone. "I'm not doing all your dirty work. I'm not going to gather them up for you and present them on a platter. I'll take you out, and then you're on your own."

"Whatever. I got one kiss already."

"You got lucky," countered Cheyenne.

"I'll send out an email with the dates and agenda for the next meeting," said Katherine out of habit, half the attendees to the meeting had already left.

Chloe came up to Katherine, wanting to talk to her about Gordy, but she faced the wall, away from her.

"Katherine? There's something I want to tell you about ..."

Katherine turned her head and was still on the phone. She mouthed, "tell me later."

"It's important," Chloe mouthed back.

Katherine's phone was on her ear. She held her hand up, palm in Chloe's face and shook her head.

Chloe mouthed the words, "really important!"

Katherine mouthed back, "Ok! This afternoon. My desk." Without another word, she walked to the other side of the room.

Chloe gathered her things brusquely. First Madeline cut her off and now Katherine. Even so, until that meeting, no one had talked about the lobbyist, and it was a critical component, at least to her. Nobody was taking her seriously yet. She'd have to find a way to make them listen to her. She had to tell Katherine about Gordy.

Chloe pulled her phone out to check email and headed out the door. She ran right into someone. Her arms flung out and her head bumped against his chest. That smell. She knew it was him before she saw him. That warm peppery musk caused her body to react with stunned pleasure. It was Harrison. In the chaos, she dropped her phone. He bent down to pick it up for her.

"Hey watch where ... Oh. Wow. It's you." He gave her that bourbon smooth smile. Underneath his cool demeanor, Chloe noticed an expression of longing.

Katherine clicked on her phone and put it down. "Where is he?" She glanced up as Harrison handed Chloe back her phone. "You two know each other.

Met yesterday, right?" Her phone rang. "Ugh shit!" she said before answering it, then walked over to a more private area in the room.

"I believe we have met," Harrison said in a low, husky voice just so Chloe could hear, "more than once."

Chloe swore his voice was genetically engineered to turn her on. But then, when he glanced over at Katherine, his expression turned professional. She was off the phone and setting up her computer for their meeting.

"Were you able to get through all those edits from our meeting?" he asked Chloe. He absentmindedly smoothed down the front of his shirt and straightened his jacket.

"I gave the finished docs to Katherine yesterday," she replied, unable to resist licking her lips.

"Good to hear. Did you watch the game last night?"

"No. I. Um. No." she responded confused.

Game? What was he talking about?

"Okay. I'll see you around?" He appeared aloof and wouldn't make eye contact with her, but Chloe swore there was a hint of desire there, that he wanted her to stay. Damn his brown eyes.

"Yeah, sure. Um. Meeting's over. Okay. See ya

later." Chloe walked towards the table. Flustered and confused as to why the table blocked her way, she looked down startled and then sighed. "Oh. Ha. Right. The door is that way."

"The door is that way," he said, grinning.

Mustering up all the confidence she could fit into her size four figure, she straightened up her spine and set a determined expression. Forget him. Harrison wasn't the only fish in this town. She was going to win this game. The hell with him and everyone else.

Chapter 6

$\mathcal{H}$arrison hated to see her leave angry. It went against every instinct he had to restrain himself. What he wanted was to chase her down and kiss those sassy lips. He wanted to bury his nose in her soft, vanilla bean scented hair.

He imagined the curve of her hips, and fantasized his fingers inside her, making her wet. His balls tightened. He was hard. Uncomfortable, he tried to imagine anything else. The Nationals playing baseball, hockey stats, but nothing worked. He couldn't leave, he had a meeting with Katherine.

Maybe they were all excuses, reasons to cover his intentions: he didn't want to mix work and play. He'd been burned before. Still, no matter how many times he tried to logically cool his body down after being near her, he couldn't. Every time he saw her, he wanted her badly. At the meeting, Harrison didn't want Katherine or Madeline to have any idea how strongly he felt for Chloe. He wanted to make sure Chloe's job wasn't threatened by his presence. So, he was strictly professional, maybe too professional.

"Harrison! I apologize for taking so long. Let's get to work," Katherine said.

"Everything is right on track. Once the changes come through, we'll review and sign off as needed. You got the changes from Chloe?" He dropped into a chair across from her.

"Yes. Yesterday. You both did a great job so far. Let's keep it up and head to the finish line."

"Chloe is doing fantastic work. She uncovered two critical issues with the doc and made invaluable edits. She has a knack for this job, I was surprised myself how good she was. It will be great to have her in Vegas."

"Only one of us is going with the Congressman to Vegas."

"Oh. And who will that be?" He pretended to show interest in the answer, but if he had to be honest ...

"We haven't decided yet." Katherine tapped her pen on the table until everyone else stopped talking.

"I'm sure you have your reasons, but Chloe should be there. This project is off to a great start because of her. She'll be a real asset on the ground."

"We'll take that into consideration." Katherine opened her notebook and began to write something down.

Harrison knew her well enough to know that further engagement on this topic would get him nowhere. "There's something else I need to tell you about. Something important."

Katherine paused from her work and looked up. "What's that?"

"Gordy. The junior Oil and Gas lobbyist? He saw Chloe and I walking to the meeting."

"Why didn't either of you mention this earlier? Ugh. Now that I think about it, that must be what Chloe was trying to tell me, but I ... this could ruin..."

"We were able to throw him off track. I felt bad, but I told him Chloe was barely an intern and there was nothing for him to worry about. I think he bought it."

Harrison felt uncomfortable calling Chloe a

lowly intern, but by doing so, he was protecting her, not hurting her.

"That man has the nose of a bloodhound. We have to throw him off, but we have to do it carefully. Permanently," Katherine said.

Harrison acquiesced. Gordy was like walking through a field of burrs, and once he knew what they were up to, he'd be like a damn runaway train. He'd seen it happen before.

"You know Congressman Bender's office? They have an intro packet for all incoming staff. In it, there are pictures of all the lobbyist and fundraisers. Every newbie is made to review and memorize the faces. Helps keep the hijinks to a minimum. You folks could use one of your own."

Katherine blinked a couple of times. "There's also a website, I believe, but it might not be official. I'll make sure Chloe has access to it or maybe I'll grab one of Bender's packets. It might be fun to compare information." She shook her head and waved away the thought with a a hand. "But, that doesn't solve our immediate problem with Gordy, and God help us if his boss gets a sniff. Krista is like a pit-bull when she gets hold of things. This shit will be off the rails before it even starts."

There was quiet in the room as they considered

the problem at hand. She shuffled papers and then suddenly, pushed back from the table.

"That's it!" she cried out.

"Oh no...I don't like the sound of *that*." Katherine had a particularly mischievous gleam in her eye he knew meant trouble.

"You have to date her Harrison. It's a perfect cover. Then, if you run into him again, you can give him some dumb excuse about being on a date, or you know, whatever you want."

"Are you suggesting *I* date her?" he replied. He wanted to, God knows he did, and it was the perfect reason to, but if she ever got wind that it was suggested in a meeting that the two of them date, she would be angrier than a hive of angry bees.

The idea of dating someone for political reasons sounded all too familiar to him. When he first got to the Hill, this woman, this gorgeous woman flirted with him, sweetened him up. He fell head over heels. Turned out though, she was looking for access and information. After she got what she wanted, his ass went straight to the curb.

"I don't know Katherine. I'm not that kind of guy. I like Chloe anyway and planned to ask her out after the job."

"Christmas came early. You don't have to fuck

her, just be her pretend boyfriend. Ask her to coffee and hold her hand," said Katherine, dragging him out of his emotional turmoil.

"And should I have pretend sex with her?" He frowned. He couldn't *pretend* date her, he was already half way in love with her. There was no way he could be a pretend boyfriend. And keeping his hands off her? Not even a remote possibility. The way Chloe affected him, he knew more would happen. He should tell Katherine it was a bad idea and say no.

"You and her, it's already a game. I probably shouldn't tell you. Chloe would kill me if she knew. And so would Madeline. But, in the interest of full disclosure, I'm going to tell you."

"Tell me what?"

"You have to promise me to keep this a secret. Can you do that?"

"You know I can."

Katherine scuffled her feet first and twisted the cap off a pen, obviously still undecided. "Alright. We're playing this game to choose who gets to go to Vegas. You have to kiss someone, five guys actually. Each at a different monument. We have customized Bingo Cards for it. The winner goes to Vegas."

Harrison sat back in his chair trying to figure out if Katherine was pulling an elaborate joke on him. But, he knew her well enough to see that she was shooting straight.

"Like the Lincoln Memorial?" he asked. It would totally explain Chloe's oddball secret mission last night.

"That's one of them, yes." Katherine tilted her head back and chuckled. "Oh, right. I saw Chloe's check-in. She's already played you. I knew that girl had some spunk. You better be careful Harrison."

"That's a fucked up game, Kat."

"Come on. It's not that bad. And don't tell anyone. If anyone ever finds out, we're toast."

"You can trust me. We've known each other a long time."

"If you date her, that will keep Gordy off our backs. Seriously, if his boss Krista thinks something real is happening, we are all fucked."

"I've been waiting a long time to see legislation like this, so it's not coming from me. I'll do it. I'll date her," he said. "But only with the following conditions. First, I am NOT dating her to cover up for Gordy. I'll date because I like her. Second, this conversation never happened."

"Sure," Katherine said, sounding sincere. Her shoulders dropped. She cocked her head, and tossed her pen onto the table. She leaned in close, examining him. "Oh my God. You really like her, don't you?"

Harrison kept her gaze and scratched his elbow. "I won't date her as a cover. If this goes south, it's your fault."

"Honey. You are from the South. It is your comfort zone. Don't worry, it'll be a little hand-holding and then you're done. A couple of days, tops."

Harrison smiled back, but didn't clarify his intentions toward Chloe to Katherine. A little hand-holding was not going to happen. If he was going to date Chloe, he was truly going to date her. Once they started, it'd be hard to stop what was coming, it'd be damn near impossible for him.

"Don't break her heart, though. I need her focused on work."

AFTER THE MEETING, Harrison wasted no time. He had to find Chloe. Immediately, he went to Link's office. Chloe was at her desk. She looked up from her work, sensing something, and saw him in the doorway. He could tell she looked confused and then anger washed over her expression. He had been trying to balance between flirting with her and keeping it professional, apparently it wasn't working.

"Darlin', I'm here to ask if you would accompany me to get coffee."

"I don't know," she said, her eyes practically sparked with anger or desire, he wasn't sure.

"Caiman. It's just coffee. Come with me."

She stayed at her desk with a resolute expression. Frankly, he wanted to take her right now, to kiss her hard, to sweep his hands around her perfect peach ass, to squeeze her perfect, hand-size breasts. He remembered how they felt against his chest. He was getting hard again. Any more of this and he'd be in physical pain. He had to focus.

Chloe.

Coffee.

She stood up without a word and put her coat on slinging her purse over her shoulder. "Just coffee?"

He held the door for her. "Just coffee. After you ma'am."

Chloe stopped right in front of him and faced

him. She put her hands on her hips. He had to forcibly restrain himself from pushing her against the wall and kissing her. She would be feisty in bed, a real caiman in the sack.

She raised one eyebrow at him. "You sure you want to get coffee with me?" Her voice was low and husky.

"Evidently. Besides, when you're with me, nothing bad can happen."

They walked down the hall. Neither of them said a word for a few minutes. Then Harrison touched the back of her shoulder closest to him. "Look Chloe. This may seem like a big city to you, that people will come and go, but on the Hill, it's a small village, complete with the town gossip, the drunk, and the whole lot of them."

"Okay..." She appeared to be appraising him still. "Why did you ask me out for coffee?"

He stopped walking. Naturally, he wasn't going to tell her the whole truth. Just like he knew she wasn't going to tell him the whole truth. But honestly, he cared about her and felt an almost instinctive need to protect her.

"I thought you might be thirsty." It was better to avoid the potentially messy conversation and stick to the basics.

"Good answer."

At the coffee shop, he ordered a café au lait and she ordered an iced tea. They sat at a table as far from other people as they could.

"Look, I'm sorry if I offended you, when Gordy was there. My intent wasn't to hurt you, just to get Gordy off our tail."

"Thank you for saying that. I do appreciate it, even if you did call me a lowly intern."

She was still smarting from the conversation. He could only apologize in so many ways, but he'd get her to see it was for her own good eventually.

"Gordy is a good guy. We were roommates in college, and belonged to the same fraternity, but now we're on different sides of the fence at work." He chuckled, almost as if he couldn't believe it. "Hell, we even play flag football on a coed team together. Maybe you want to come with me. The game's tonight."

"Didn't you tell him you couldn't make it?" she asked, her guard back up again.

"Do you remember every single thing ever spoken?"

"Pretty much. I've had to. This town is crazy. I mean, I never even thought it would be anything like this when I studied history in high school."

"Context is important."

"I remember my Grandma telling me the phrase Do Nothing Congress was coined back in 1948."

"I didn't know that. Truman. Huh. Some things don't change. So, would you like to join me in a game of flag football tonight? Roundabout 6:30 p.m.?"

She didn't look particularly thrilled with the idea. "Sure."

"We can always use an extra on the field. We can go out for a beer afterwards."

"Tonight? Coed flag football?" She was a little tired, but her curiosity was piqued. "Okay. I'll do it."

"Nice! We'll definitely win with a caiman on the team."

"Harrison," she said, mock-hitting his shoulder.

He caught Chloe's hand. Harrison had grown up hustling the back streets of New Orleans. Being physically fast was a necessity to save your life. He caressed her palm lightly with his thumb.

"You are fast as a flash," she said.

"I am good at what I do."

"I don't doubt that, not for one single second."

He pressed his fingers between hers so they were fully embraced, for just a minute. Her hand was warm, soft, but the fingers strong. He noticed she kept her fingernails short, but they were manicured.

"I'll email you with the particulars." He said before letting her hand fall away, "I'll see you tonight for the game?"

"I've never played flag football before."

"I'm sure you'll have no trouble, Caiman."

Chapter 7

Cheyenne had emailed her twenty minutes ago, saying she needed a caffeine fix, and Chloe replied with a 'yes' and they'd meet in a half hour. She was glad for the break. The air conditioning was down and it was hot as a lambing shed in July. Reading law precedents and other legalese did not help, and her eyelids kept slamming shut. Even with the excitement of seeing Harrison again in an hour or so, she kept nodding off at her desk.

What she wanted to do was talk to someone about Harrison and Gordy. She trusted Cheyenne who was, without fail, direct. Sometimes it was a shock to her, especially to her Midwestern view of communication styles, but at least she never had to figure out the underlying message, she got the truth plain and simple. Also, since Cheyenne was relatively the same age, and in the same kind of job position, Chloe knew her advice would naturally include those factors.

The coffee shop in the basement of the Cannon building was empty. Nobody was in there this late in the day, and it smelled of coffee grounds and stale pastry. Cheyenne had not yet arrived. Chloe wanted something special besides her usual drip and ordered an iced vanilla latte to help cool her off and wake her up.

Cheyenne breezed in. "Thanks for meeting me. It's so hot in this building, I thought I was going to die. I wanted to curl up under my desk and take a nap in the shade."

"No kidding. Do you think they'll ever get around to fixing the air conditioning?"

"I don't know, but I wish to Hades and back that more people would use deodorant."

"Is it that bad?"

"The smell of constant adrenaline and covert fear is always in the house."

Chloe chuckled. She liked Cheyenne and her sense of humor. While Cheyenne ordered, she sat down and sipped on her latte, grateful for the icy chill in her body.

"So guess who stopped by the office," Chloe said when Cheyenne had situated herself.

"The hot guy you left the bar with?"

"Yes. So, get this, turns out he is working on the project with us. Yesterday, I had to work with him. He's the environmental attorney for the Vegas project."

"What?" With the shocked look on her face, even Chloe had to smile, not much got that kind of reaction out of her. "Shut the front door!"

"He was my first BINGO kiss. And," she paused, "we even had coffee, here, earlier today. He invited me to play flag football with him tonight."

"You are kidding!"

"I am not." She held up two fingers. "Scouts honor."

"Are you going?" Cheyenne asked. She sipped at her coffee. "And the bigger question ... if you go out with him, are you going to keep playing this game?"

"I don't know. I mean, it's too early to know, with him. And I want to go to Vegas. This opportunity is career changing."

"For a couple of kisses, it's a huge payout. Madeline and Katherine can't be liking this game."

"Madeline came up with the game. She probably came up with this game so she could win. But Katherine, no way she likes it. It bugs her. And Liz? I can't even imagine what she thinks."

"I noticed Opal doesn't have any check in's either.".

"I was flabbergasted by her," said Chloe. "I mean, Opal has a degree from freaking Harvard, and she lets people treat her like this?"

"She graduated from Harvard? I didn't know. Maybe she is incredibly smart, but doesn't have great social skills. It's weird, she's weird."

"Poor Opal."

"She's always with Link too. Think they are up to something?"

"She doesn't look like the type a Congressman would go for," Chloe said sipping her drink.

"Anyway, back to Harrison. Are you going to try and find someone to kiss for the next letter?"

"Sure. I guess. Why not. It's not like Harrison and I are a couple. Besides, Madeline already has three kisses. How?"

"That woman has it locked down. I wouldn't be surprised if she wins. So, that means it is time to get down and dirty. Either you start getting some more BINGO letters or you stick with Harrison. And well, what you said is spot on. Harrison isn't a sure thing."

Chloe gave her friend a weak smile. She wanted more than anything to go to Vegas, but she also knew that someone like Harrison didn't come along very often.

Harrison rang for her at her apartment. When she came down to meet him, he was standing in front of a 1973 Scout. Maybe they should have taken the Metro to the Mall, but now she understood why Harrison wanted to drive so badly. She imagined he had driven the vehicle across muddy hills of Louisiana just to get to the best fishing holes. Harrison kissed her cheek, and, with a flourish, opened the passenger door.

"Welcome to my ride," he said with a goofy grin.

"Nice rig. I'm impressed." It was taller than she expected, and she lifted her foot into the door and with her other hand grabbed a handle. He clasped her waist and helped propel her into the vehicle.

"Scout's seen more crawdad boils than you know," he said, shutting the door.

Harrison started the SUV and the whole vehicle rumbled. They headed towards the Mall, where they would be playing their game. She had to remind herself they were not going to a shopping mall, but that Mall also meant a sheltered walk, or a promenade. To get a breeze, she turned the window handle to roll down the window, but it was tougher than she thought, and she had to add a little elbow grease to get it open.

The scent of the city flew in, a clash of exhaust fumes, cherry blossoms, mingled with a primordial smell of river banks. It was very different from the hay infused air she smelled when growing up, but she liked both. She could be a city girl and a country mouse, why not both? Why choose?

The cool wind blew her hair about, and she tracked it down and pulled it into a pony tail. He put his arm across the back of the seat, and she let her pony swing over his arm. In response, he tickled the back of her neck.

"Harrison, why are your hands so rough?" she asked.

He pulled his hand out from behind her and laid

it in her lap. She turned it so that the palm was facing up.

"I used to work construction when I was a kid. Fifteen years old and I was hammering away at doors and building walls for the rich folks in the French Quarter. Met my first lawyer there. He sort of inspired me."

She rubbed the callous with her thumb, and smiled at him.

"I know hard work. I was raised on a farm. Maybe someday I'll show you the best way to toss a hay bale."

"Damn, Caimon. Is there anything you can't do? I'd love to see you toss a hay bale, but first, how's your ball game? Can you toss a ball?"

"Sure. I can do anything I put my mind to," she said with a charming smile.

When they arrived at the Mall, most of the vehicles were headed down 12th street, to get out of town and home to Virginia. Luckily, they found a parking spot after going around only once. The game would be played on the National Mall. *The National Mall!* Smack dab between the National History Museum and the maroon Smithsonian Institution Castle. In front of her was the Capital building. Of all the things she imagined she'd do in DC, playing flag football here on the Mall, which she always thought would be cordoned off. She loved that the city was open to its residents, not all privatized and restricted. There was a certain irony that she relished in playing a game in front of the Capital.

There was already a group of people standing around waiting for the game to start. She could tell they knew each other with their easy camaraderie. A white mesh bag half spilled the footballs and bright orange flag tags onto the ground. Nearby were a few red coolers filled with water and soda.

She had worn soccer shorts, they were loose enough, but tight in the right areas. Gordy was out on the field, doing a hamstring stretch. She had to admit that he was good looking, that dark red hair of his was oddly mesmerizing. Gordy finished his stretch and put his foot down, then waved to Harrison. He shifted his gaze and took a long look at Chloe, ending with a wink. Harrison stiffened and cocked his head.

"Hey Harrison! Good to see you man, and I like the package you brought."

"Knock it off Gordy. It's not funny. You ready to play today? Who's got the lead?"

"Jenny does, she's setting up the roster and positions now. There are t-shirts over there. You'll need to change in order to play." He turned to Chloe, giving her a slow up and down with his brilliant green eyes.

Harrison hit Gordy in the chest, somewhat playing, somewhat serious. "Give it a rest dirtbag."

"Alright alright, come this way ladies and gentlemen, we enter the arena!" He threw his hands up in the air and hummed a cheering crowd.

Chloe had to laugh. He was full of himself, charming in his own unique way. No wonder women fell for him, if they liked the jerky kind of guy. Some women were attracted to that, they knew Gordy would not hold back. She couldn't believe she had even considered him for a BINGO kiss, but maybe that was all he was good for anyway. He didn't seem the type who would ever have a relationship, only fast women. To each their own. If that was what a woman wanted, so be it. She just knew she didn't want that kind of man in her life. Still though, she couldn't help but feel like she wanted to talk to him.

Jenny was nice. She had a kind smile, brunette hair, and blue eyes. She handed her a new t-shirt and called over some of the girls. They circled around her to make a shield while Chloe slipped off her shirt and put the new t-shirt on. They were far enough away from the Metro entrance that people wouldn't see, and besides, most of the people were too busy on their phones to even notice the split second it took for her to change.

Gordy called the huddle up and explained the play. Jenny was the quarterback, she had an amazing throw, having played fast-pitch softball and winning a regional tournament. She'd pass it to Harrison who would run it in for a touchdown.

Everyone lined up. The ref blew the whistle. Jenny scooted back and the rest of the team bolted forward. The other team piled around Gordy, he couldn't get free, but Harrison was wide open. Jenny snapped the ball to him. Gordy, seeing what was about to happen, broke through the people holding him and leaped up in the air to make the catch. The ball landed safely in his outstretched arms. He hugged it and landed on the ground with a thud.

Harrison looked pissed. He held a helping hand down to Gordy. "Way to make the play."

"I didn't think you'd make it buddy. Don't be mad, it's for the team you know."

"I coulda had it."

Gordy smirked. "Shoulda, woulda, coulda."

Jenny rolled her eyes at him, but Harrison and Chloe gave him a dirty look. For the next play, they didn't huddle up. Jenny explained that she'd just throw it to whoever was open. The whistle blew and the team scrambled to different areas of the field.

Chloe ran straight ahead and turned to face Jenny, and saw that the ball was already half way to her. She brought up her hands to catch the ball and it thumped hard in her chest. She staggered, but didn't fall, and blindly headed for the touchdown zone.

Gordy was right by her side, trying to block off other players. One of them sacked Gordy, and he fell right into Chloe, taking her down with him. She felt his arms go around her in a bear hug as they tumbled to the ground. When they stopped sliding on the ground, he opened his eyes first.

"Chloe?" asked Gordy.

"Yes. Let me go?" The football had smashed against her chest a lot harder than she had expected and now the area was smarting. The crash landing to the ground made her hips hurt and her knee throb. The bear hug didn't make anything feel better, but she wasn't focused on the pain. His eyes were locked onto hers. The different shades of green seemed to call her like a siren's song.

"Are you okay?" he asked, smiling at her, like he was just a nice young man helping a friend out. He stood up and offered her a hand. She took the offer and he helped her up. Maybe he wasn't such a bad guy after all.

"Chloe. You okay?" asked Harrison.

"I think so. That football hit harder than I thought," she said rubbing her chest. The sting blossomed into a sharp pain. "The catching part looks so easy when you watch it on TV."

"It's pretty brutal. You want to sit the next one out?"

"Um, yeah, I kinda do. I'm … yeah, this hurts."

"Sure. Hey Jen, Chloe's out for the next round, okay?"

Jenny tilted her head apologetically. "Sorry dude. She can't, we don't have enough players. If she steps out, we have to forfeit."

"Okay, then I'll stay in the game. It doesn't hurt that bad." She was lying through her teeth, but she didn't want Harrison to think she was a complete wimp.

The huddle was led by Jenny. She called a generic play that whoever was open, was the person she would throw to, of course with the exception of Chloe, who could just guard.

In the lineup, Chloe didn't even bother to look at Gordy, she kept her focus on Jenny. The whistle blew and the center snapped the ball to her. She scanned the field and threw it to Harrison, who seemed to be in a pocket. Right behind him, Gordy ran for the ball. Harrison leapt up and pushed off Gordy. He caught the ball in his fingers, clutching onto it and bringing it into his chest. Gordy fell backwards and landed on the ground with a thud.

Harrison ran for the zone. Chloe jumped up and down, yelling at him to run. She had never been so excited watching a man run with a football before. Her chest started throbbing again, and she wrapped her arms around her ribs. *He can make it. He can get the touchdown.* And -- he does! The team mates cheer, and run to him with hands up for a high five.

Gordy stood up and slapped the dust from his shorts.

"I don't know what kind of play that was Harrison, but I'm onto you now."

The smile erased from Harrison's face and he turned to stare at Gordy. "What the hell are you talking about?"

"That was a shitty move Harrison. I want you to know, I'm coming after you now."

Harrison turned and fast as a flash, ran towards Gordy and tackled him with his shoulders. The two of them went flying into the air and scrambled around on the ground.

"Knock it off!" yelled Chloe into the dusty pair, unsure if either of them could hear her.

Jenny kicked Gordy's shoe hard. "Get your ass up and stop this shit or I'm kicking you both out of the league. This is bullshit!" She finished with a swift kick to Harrison's foot too.

Gordy and Harrison split up, both red-faced and breathing hard.

Gordy put his hands on his knees, trying to catch his breath and started laughing. "Harrison! Helluva tackle brother!" Then he directed his gaze at Harrison. It looked deadly, as if he had him perfectly lined up in a scope. "Watch yourself, bro.." He slapped his knee again with a humorless laugh.

Harrison barely smiled, his expression wary of Gordy. Chloe wasn't sure what had just happened, but she knew that she had to be careful of Gordy. She had better watch her back at work, too.

She'd need to tell Katherine, make sure that she knew Gordy was snooping around. If this was just a preview of Gordy's game tactics, she was afraid to know what he'd be like when the game was full on.

Chapter 9

Harrison completely understood when Chloe wanted to go home after the football game. Her chest still hurt, and after the skirmish with Gordy, there was no chance of any romance. He knew it. She knew it. He lifted her out of the Scout, kissing her lightly before she hobbled away toward her apartment.

The next morning, he meant to text her first thing, but he'd been busy in and out of meetings all day that he barely had time to go to the bathroom, let alone text. Glancing at his watch, he was surprised that it was already ten. He headed towards the Cannon Building for a meeting that didn't involve the Pierce team. He was about to text Chloe to let her know he would be there when Gordy yelled at him from across the lawn.

"Hey Harrison! Wait up man!" He ran across the grass to catch up. Out of breath, he put both hands on his knees, "Whoo! Great game last night."

"You're getting old Gordy. Need to work on your cardio."

"Oh man. Don't I know it. Hey. Sorry about your girl. Turns out you just like her too, right? She's hot. What's not to like."

"Come off it, Gordy. Lay off."

"I didn't know you were *with* her, man. Lighten up."

"That never stops you, does it? We've known each other a long time. You'd hit on her whether or not you think I liked her."

"You're right there. How long has it been Harrison? Five years since we graduated? Ten years since we met?"

"A day I'll never forget."

"Remember? You were working as a cashier at the student union. I didn't have my ID with me, but you let me have my discount anyway."

Harrison nodded in response, it was Gordy's way of reminding him that he came from money, while Harrison had to work hard for everything he had, including work-study to get through school.

"Time flies. Anyway, Chloe is no dice. Cold as ice."

"You sound like an idiot." Chloe was anything but cold.

"The ladies love me Harrison, always have. Don't forget it. By the way, I got my eyes on you two." Gordy clapped him on the shoulder.

"I've got a call to make," said Harrison. "Why don't you go on ahead. I'll catch up with you later."

"Sure Harrison," he said. Gordy waved and headed into Cannon. "I'm meeting up with Krista. We're keeping an eye on Chloe too." He chuckled, though Harrison had no idea what the joke might be. "Just thought I'd give you a head's up first. Consider it a token of respect."

Harrison waved him off, there was no point in getting into a conversation with him. Gordy *was* an idiot, but not someone to be dismissed. He shouldn't have brought Chloe to the game last night, the thought of unintentionally harming her made him feel ill.

Harrison genuinely liked women, he thought they were smart and sexy. Gordy tended to treat them like some kind of commodity. He was a player who didn't care about who he slept with, and he slept with a lot of them, most of them young and fresh in DC.

Ever since he became a lobbyist, he played harder and faster than ever before. A great way to get info, he had once said. Gordy and Harrison had been good friends in college, but over the years, he distanced himself from Gordy. The thin lines of their history kept the friendship together, but even that link was close to breaking.

Harrison pulled out his phone and pressed Chloe's number. It went to voice mail.

"Hey Chloe. It's me. I would have called sooner, but I had meetings all morning. I hope you feel better today. If you're up to it, let me know, maybe we can do something this weekend? Call me back."

He hung up the phone. There was a chill in the air and he tightened his jacket before heading inside.

Chapter 10

$\mathcal{C}$hloe's morning did not go well. First, she overslept and missed a key morning meeting. She decided to skip her regular stop at the neighborhood coffee shop, so instead of being in a good mood and ready to work when she got to the office, she was sluggish and irritable.

Then, as she went through security, a guard stopped her and she had to spend fifteen minutes going through a specialized search. She never found out why--just the stars were not aligned properly today and her crappy morning was the result. Her chest still hurt from catching the football at the game the night before. She rubbed her pectoral muscles tenderly, no wonder football players have such well-developed muscles there.

Congressman Lincoln Ulysses Pierce was the first person to greet her as she walked into the office. He looked sharp today, as usual, with a navy-blue pinstripe suit and a white button down. His power tie was a solid purple, the color of royalty. She wondered if he had a personal shopper who helped him select the color based on psychological data or if he just liked purple.

"Hey Chloe, welcome to the office," he said, flashing her a deep smile.

"Sorry Mr. Link, I mean Congressman Pierce, I'll pull up your constituent list right away."

"Mr. Link," he said, "I like it. It sounds like a CIA cover or a video game name. I'm going to reprint my business cards." He held his hands up in the air to accentuate the words, "Mr. Link."

"Ha ha. You're funny. Sorry I was late. I played flag football last night and I caught one of the balls. Wow, I didn't think it would hurt that bad."

"That can be brutal. I was always sore after a game. Tonight, get yourself one of those medicated stickies, they really help."

"That's a good idea, thanks. It'll just take a few minutes for me to get things updated. If you need to work, I can bring it in when I'm finished."

"You do that Ms. Cassell. I'll see you in thirty

minutes or so?"

"That sounds about right, sir."

Chloe started the compilation which didn't take her very long since most of the correspondence was e-mail rather than snail mail. She was so focused on her work she didn't notice Opal standing in front of her desk. After a few minutes, Opal cleared her throat noisily.

"So what happened this morning Chloe? Any reason as to why you're late?"

Chloe looked up and was frankly shocked that Opal would talk to her that way. She was usually mousy and asking how she could help.

"Not that it's any of your business?"

"We can't have this kind of behavior at the office, I mean, you've got to be on time. We missed you at the morning meeting and you almost missed the deadline for the constituent list."

"Are you scolding me?" asked Chloe, her eyes having gone from round orbs to narrow slits.

"Step up your game. You're at a Congressional Office, not some frat house. You need to arrive on time."

Before Chloe could respond, Opal spun away and stormed out of the office.

"What in the..." said Chloe under her breath.

"She always gets that way when it comes to Link," said Madeline from across the small room. "I don't know what it is, but do not mess with her. She's like a momma bear if it has anything to do with him." She tipped her head towards his office.

"And that's okay?" asked Chloe. "She's not even my boss. She shouldn't be telling me what to do."

"Her hard work ethic and output is so high and of such quality caliber that Carleen and Katherine overlook the issue."

"The upside is it doesn't happen much?"

"Depends. If something goes wrong in the middle of a voting cycle, watch out. Even I have been at the brunt of her wrath. It's kind of cute."

Chloe wasn't sure Opal and wrathful went together. She sure hadn't looked at all 'cute' two minutes ago. "You don't mind?"

"Nah. It's never personal. And usually it's true," she said looking at her with a smile.

Chloe couldn't tell if she was smirking or what, but the words stung. The comment hung in the air. Chloe shifted uncomfortably in her seat, but instead of addressing Madeline, she went to work and started typing away on her computer. Her goal was to finish the constituent list, hand it over and get the hell out of there for a coffee.

Within fifteen minutes, she had compiled the list and triple checked it for accuracy. Then, she emailed it to the Congressman with a cc to Opal. She had also sent a copy to the printer. As soon as the document was printed, she picked it up and walked into Link's office. He was on the phone, so she set it in his work basket. He gave her a thumbs up.

She went to her desk and picked up her purse. She paused in front of Madeline. "I'm headed to the coffee shop. Do you want anything?"

"No. I'm fine, I'm headed out of here anyways for a luncheon. And Chloe?"

"Yeah?"

"Don't stress about it. Everyone has one of those days."

"Thanks Madeline. I'll see you later."

Chloe was almost to the coffee shop when she saw Gordy leaning against the wall. Next to him was a woman. She wore a tailored power suit in black with very expensive pumps, and a chic Diane von Furstenberg shirt. Gordy saw her, turned and leaned close to the other woman, covering his mouth. It was totally obvious he was talking about her. It was too late to turn around, so she straightened her back and clenched her jaw.

Gordy turned and caught her eye again. With a smile, he raised his hand and waved her over. "Hey Chloe! Come on over here. I want to introduce you to someone."

"Sure Gordy," she said, tapping her watch for emphasis. "I don't have much time, I have a meeting in ten minutes."

"This will be worth it, I promise." His green eyes were dancing, as if this was fun for him. "This is Krista Ellis, she's my boss and director at our firm-- Porter and Associates."

"Hi Krista, nice to meet you," she said, offering as little as possible.

Krista studied her, and she suddenly felt like a wounded seal in shark territory.

"Gordy tells me you've been meeting up with Harrison, spending some time with him?" she asked with a sweet smile that opposed the menacing look in her eyes.

Did they teach that look at Lobbyist Class 101?

"Why would you care if Harrison and I spend time together? I'm just an intern. It's not like I do anything important."

"But you are important. Without interns, nothing would get done. You are like the blood vessels of this giant beast."

"Thanks. I guess. Is that all? I have to ..."

"We are just curious what specific legislation you're working on with Harrison?"

At least it was a direct question. Chloe knew if she tried to throw them off with a 'mind your own business' the sharks would circle in closer. She didn't dare mention a word about SUNFLOWER, the secret meeting the Congressman had set up in Vegas.

But, for the moment, she didn't know what to say, she felt stunned, as if they were trying to knock her off her game. She looked at her phone to buy some time for an answer. The office meeting schedule popped up. Thankfully, it wouldn't show anything about SUNFLOWER on there. It would be regular staff meetings.

She glanced up and would have sworn Krista and Gordy were on the verge of drooling.

"Everything Congressman Pierce is working on is public information, why don't you just look it up?" She thought about misdirecting them elsewhere, but honestly, she didn't want to. The results could be catastrophic and the last thing Chloe wanted was to become a casualty intern. She had heard about them in law school. The ones who caved, the ones who were tagged with an unfavorable label, the ones who couldn't cut it. Chloe clenched her teeth and squared her shoulders. The hell with them, she wasn't going to give either of them a single iota of data.

"Interesting. Harrison works in environmental law. And only environmental law. As far as I know there's nothing going on in that area in Congressman Pierce's purview," Krista said, her voice a smooth satin alto. "It makes no sense that he'd be spending time with one of the congressman's interns unless the congressman is drafting new, as yet unreleased, legislation."

Chloe blinked at the woman. Should she play the 'we're dating card'? That might be too obvious. Instead, she shrugged and smiled. "I came down to get coffee before my meeting. If you don't mind."

She tried stepping around the two lobbyists, but Gordy stretched his arm out as if he were just leaning against the wall effectively blocking her way.

"We are working to make sure that Oil and Gas is involved in any long-term legislation. You know, you could benefit greatly by working with us, not against us. I know you're a second-year law student. We could certainly arrange some things for you. Help you with those student loans of yours."

Chloe stepped back. Nothing had prepared her

for this bald-faced approach that greased the political wheel. Had they researched her? Or was it just that common knowledge every law student racked up to 180K in debt?

"Like I said, all my work is available to the public. You can see on the roster who I'm meeting with and pretty much, with an educated guess, figure out what I'm working on."

"If it's that easy, then just tell us," said Gordy. "What's the big deal?"

He was right. Chloe could feel fear rising in her belly. The look crossed her face, she could tell because Krista smiled suddenly, as if she had succeeded in hunting her prey. But Chloe recognized the fear as the same feeling she'd get just before a barrel race, and knew how to quash it.

She came back on the offensive. "The big deal is both of you are unable to make educated guesses. You're just fishing. If you have something specific you'd like to talk to me about then let's hear it."

Both Krista and Gordy were quiet. There was blood in the water now. There was a weighted silence between the three of them, but then Krista cleared her throat. She started to laugh.

"Oh my god, Chloe. You are fantastic! We could really use someone like you on the team. I'm serious about that offer. You'd make more money in one month on my team than you would a whole year as a staffer. Here's my card."

Chloe regarded the business card before taking it, and glared at Gordy. Working for a lobbyist firm was something she had considered as a career trajectory, part of the reason she wanted so badly to be on the SUNFLOWER project. She glanced around the hallway to make sure no one she knew was there, and took the card.

Gordy and Krista gave each other a quick look.

"I have to get coffee and lunch. I'm probably going to be late for my next meeting. Thanks, you two. Nice meeting." She walked up to Gordy's outstretched arm and met his eyes, daring him to not move it. He slowly dropped his arm so she could pass. She held her head high and back straight as she rounded a corner into the coffee shop. As soon as she was out of their sight, she relaxed her shoulders and started to breathe again. Chloe had to make sure Katherine knew the sharks were circling, but she certainly didn't need to know they'd offered her a job.

It was the end of the work day. Hill staffers packed into the Capital Bar and Lounge. It smelled of pizza and beer. The festive mood was hard to appreciate for Chloe even if she was here to blow off steam from a long day. Chloe had tried to catch up with Katherine all afternoon, to let her know about Gordy and Krista, but kept missing her. When she called, her phone went to voicemail.

I could make more money in one month than an entire year as a staffer.

The offer was tempting. Most of her law school peers followed that same predictable path in politics: intern, staffer, lobbyist. She knew Harrison could help her. She texted him that she was free and would be at the Capital Bar with Cheyenne if he was interested in stopping by. He texted that he was busy, but would let her know. She hadn't heard back from him, but she wasn't worried.

Chloe stood near the door and scanned the crowd. She saw familiar faces, people she passed in the hall or bumped into in the cafeteria. Cheyenne waved to her from the middle of the bar. She had scored a two-top standing table.

Chloe wanted to give her an update on Harrison and Gordy, the football game, and Krista. She trusted Cheyenne, who was, without fail, direct in her advice. At least Chloe never had to figure out the underlying message, she got the truth plain and simple.

Also, since Cheyenne was relatively the same age, and in the same kind of job position, Chloe knew her advice would naturally include those factors. She wasn't sure if she should tell her about the job offer though, at least not until Katherine knew about it. Or, maybe, she wouldn't tell anyone at all. Her coworkers might take the information the wrong way and they might not think she was one of them.

"I took the liberty of ordering you a white wine

off the happy hour menu. You had one last time we were here."

"Nice of you, thanks." Chloe wasn't in the mood for wine. She wanted a whiskey, but she didn't change the order, she had more pressing items on her mind and wine would be alright. "So guess who I ran into today."

"Ooo la la. The hot Southern guy." Cheyenne said giving Chloe a mocking look, but with a smile.

"I wish. Gordy. The oil and gas lobbyist. And his boss, Krista."

"What?" With the shocked look on her face, even Chloe had to smile.

"I kept trying to tell Katherine," she paused, "but I can't get ahold of her. I didn't say a word about anything, but these two are circling the waters."

"Definitely tell Katherine, especially since Krista showed up. How'd the game go yesterday?" Cheyenne asked. She took a drink of her wine, "And the bigger question ... are you going to keep playing BINGO?"

"That's the other thing I wanted to tell you. I went to that flag football game, you know, and Gordy practically tackled me. Then Harrison tackled Gordy. Holy crap. I get the feeling that Harrison likes me."

"You think?" asked Cheyenne with more sarcasm than curiosity.

"I don't know. I wish I had like a magic sign that popped up over Harrison's head, 'He's the one!'"

"Yeah, I know. My kisses so far have been just that, kisses. Nothing special."

"That reminds me, how is your cooking class going?" asked Chloe.

"Pastry. Not cooking. It doesn't start until Saturday," added Cheyenne picking out the peanuts from a nut bowl and popping them in her mouth.

"I can't cook or do pastry."

"If you want to learn how to make a killer pie, you should come with me, there's a spot open. It'll be fun."

"Hey there ladies. You enjoying the evening?" asked a man's deep voice. Chloe and Cheyenne looked up. Two typical Cap Hill guys were standing across from them. They both wore white button-down shirts with no suit jackets, cropped hair, and eager expressions. They had the same coloring, and, at first glance, the only difference between them was one wore a green tie, the other an amber one. She didn't want to talk to them, but Cheyenne seemed interested.

"Sure we are. I love this happy hour." Cheyenne grinned at them in open invitation.

Chloe thought both guys were good looking. Not Harrison good looking, but at least Gap model cute.

"What're your names?" asked green tie.

"Cheyenne. I work on the Hill. Do you have a business card?" she asked. Chloe smiled in surprise. Cheyenne was going to score a third kiss tonight, she was sure of it.

"Yes ma'am." He saluted her like a fresh Marine recruit snapping to attention. "Here you go," he said and handed her a cream-colored card.

Amber-tie pulled one out of his pocket.

Cheyenne studied them both and half-smiled. She slyly winked at Chloe, and said in a low voice, "You still playing? They qualify."

"What did you say?" asked Greenie in a half-joking voice. "Are you whispering about us?"

"Yes. I am whispering about you. What kind of girl do you think I am?" she countered, teasing him with a frank smile.

The man chuckled, he seemed to approach it like a challenge. "Name's Peter. My friend here is Mike. Pleasure to meet you."

Cheyenne rested her gaze back on Chloe, waiting on an answer from her.

Chloe responded in a non-committal shrug. "Let's have fun."

Cheyenne waved at their tiny table inviting them to put their drinks down. "Peter and Mike. You are approved. For now."

"Peter! How are you man?" The voice boomed and sounded too familiar.

She saw the red hair first. It was Gordy. She tried to contain her shock. He really was a good-looking man. His skin was cream colored, and looked incredible against his copper beard. If he wasn't a guy, if he wasn't Gordy for that matter, she'd ask what moisturizer he used. She saw the reaction on Cheyenne's face too, but she covered it well.

"I think we got off on the wrong foot," he said, directing his attention to Chloe. "I always get a little competitive when I'm around Harrison and lovely ladies who are new in town."

"I'm not new to DC. I am new to the Hill. I love being an intern." Chloe said to Gordy, with sarcasm and a bit of sincerity. "I'm a second-year law student. GW."

"Impressive. What do you want to be when you grow up little girl?" Gordy asked. She looked up at him and found all of them staring at her.

She assumed a dreamy but serious look, one she

imagined a top ten pageant contestant might have, "I plan to save the world, one lobbyist at a time."

Gordy chuckled. "That is funny. How did your meeting go with Harrison?"

"I'm just an intern, remember? We met about dumb edits for existing legislation. Ugh. That's about as fun as running coffee. I know I've got to pay my dues, but still."

"The coffee runs. I remember those. I too was an intern, once."

Cheyenne and the two guys started talking. Something about going up to the beach in Delaware. Chloe's feet were tired so she leaned in towards the table and put her elbow on it. Gordy must have taken it as a sign. He moved in closer and touched her waist lightly. She pulled away and gave him a dirty look.

"Come on Chloe. We have a lot in common. We'd have fun." He touched her arm. His expression seemed to be sincere, so she relaxed.

"Harrison tells me you two have known each other awhile."

"We were assigned roommates at Tulane. Good man." Gordy stepped towards her again, about a forearm's length from her. He gestured to her, inviting her in, as if he was about to tell her a secret.

She thought of the witch inviting Hansel and Gretel into her gingerbread house, but leaned in anyway.

"WHAT THE HELL are you doing Gordy?" said Harrison.

Gordy stepped back and put his hands in the air, as if he was about to be arrested. Chloe took a deep breath. Just hearing his voice caused her to sweat. Her whole body tuned towards him, like an antenna. She was past wanting a kiss, she wanted him, all of him. And so far, all she had was...One. Fucking. Kiss.

"Harrison? What the fuck?" said Gordy.

"Hands off my girl."

"When did that happen?" Gordy looked down at Chloe to see how she would respond. Chloe merely looked back and forth between the two men, then she got up and stood slightly behind Harrison. Her heart was beating so hard she swore it was about to rip right out of her chest.

"Back off Gordy. Can't you see. She doesn't want to be with you." Harrison was about to spring on Gordy. His muscles were tense, his gaze intense and immovable. His hands curled in, ready to take a punch or defend himself if necessary.

"Why don't you ask Chloe that. She seems to be okay with our situation."

Chloe looked up at Gordy. His eyes, which had been a beguiling green just last night looked hard as slate today. She nearly recoiled from him, but was able to keep herself in check. If she had to choose between the two of them, it would definitely be Harrison.

But, she wanted to make sure the possibility of getting a job with Porter and Associates wasn't ruined either. She lowered her eyes and refused to look at Harrison, she didn't want him to see her guilty expression.

"Okay Romeo. I got the hint." Gordy said roughly, then he faced Chloe."You and me Chloe. We could be something real special at Porter and Associates. We can still offer you a position. Don't you forget that."

Harrison didn't move, but his eyes bored into her. Cheyenne was busy talking to Peter and Mike; it was clear she wasn't paying attention. She glowered at Gordy. Yes, he might be good looking, but he was one of those guys, a guy who would dine and dash, and not give it a second thought. Her gut had been right all along.

She took a gulp of air, not realizing until then she'd been holding her breath. "I won't forget Gordy. Thanks for the reminder."

Gordy stood his ground, not moving. No one moved. Then Gordy gave a *humphf* and stomped off to the bar, presumably to order another drink.

She didn't want to, but she looked up to meet Harrison's eyes and swallowed hard.

"Are you okay?" Harrison asked, not asking about what Gordy had said regarding the job offer. Did he not hear that part or was he just playing dumb for the moment?

"Yes. Thank you for saving me. That's twice now. Or is it three times?"

"You're welcome, Caiman. There are several ways to show your appreciation, if you're so inclined." He stood back, his shoulders squared, and his chin down.

When he licked his lips, she understood that soon, she was in for much more than a kiss. *Thank the Lord I wore my good panties today.* Her body responded to his Alpha male, and flooded with wet desire. Her lacy thong was uncomfortable between her thighs, pressing against her clitoris, slightly egging her on. She tried to move her hips, to move it against her, away from her, but it was firmly lodged in place.

"You're coming with me," he said.

Her body felt chilled, attuned to the barest of his movements. He reached for her hand and squeezed it. Then, he looked straight into her eyes. There would be no turning back after this.

"Now."

She caught her breath and nodded in agreement. A ripple went down her spine, and ended in her core, pulsing inside of her, an intense need to have him.

"I have to let Cheyenne know I'm leaving."

He nodded. Cheyenne was on the other side of the room, talking with Peter. He noticed and caught her attention. Chloe gave Cheyenne the OK sign. Cheyenne responded with a hand gesture that meant to call her. Chloe nodded. Harrison pulled her towards him. Her breasts brushed against his arm, and even though it hurt, her nipples turned into hard little cherry buds. He smiled at her, which seemed both protective and mischievous.

Chapter 12

While waiting for a cab, Harrison ran his hand down her back and to her waist, pulling her hips towards him. His body heat flamed against her, warming her, inciting her. As Chloe climbed into the yellow cab, her lace thong slipped and pinched against her. She quivered a little as she sat down. She wanted to rip the damn thing off and throw it out the window. Harrison reached over and slid off her bra strap. It fell down against her arm. His fingers skimmed across her breasts, tracing the outline of her nipple through her bra.

He lowered his head to her and whispered, "I like it when you watch." He slipped his fingers inside her bra, pinching her nipple between his thumb and forefinger. She gasped. Her eyes furtively moved to the rear-view mirror and Harrison pinched her harder, his fingers holding tight.

He pointed to his eyes. "Don't look anywhere else."

He let go and her nipple ached from the release. A small whimper escaped her lips. Harrison's other finger moved to his lips in a shushing sign. He slowly pulled up her skirt, and caressed her inner thighs, teasing her by stopping short of touching her aching pussy.

Every time he came close, he stopped short of giving her what she wanted. Every single movement made her weak, hungrier for more. She pressed her legs as wide as the skirt's material would give, inviting him in for a deeper exploration, wishing he would touch her one special spot.

She was pretty sure she would explode into an orgasm more powerful than the one she'd had the other night when she'd been alone without him actually touching her clit. How could that be possible?

She forgot about the driver and closed her eyes, leaning back in the seat. She felt a pinch on her thigh, and Harrison indicated her eyes shouldn't leave his. The intimacy of holding his gaze was something she had not known could be possible.

The cab slowed down. Chloe closed her legs trying to capture his hand, not wanting this moment to end. He chuckled and slid his hand free before pulling her skirt back down.

"Almost, Caiman."

He paid the driver and got out of the cab. Maybe she should stop here. She could still walk away from him and have a fighting chance to finish out the BINGO game and get to Vegas. He held his hand out for her and she took it. *Too late now*. There was only desire for Harrison. He pulled her out of the cab and helped her steady herself on her feet.

She felt as if she'd ran a 10K. She was out of breath, but she was not out of energy. And she was hungry. Being with him wasn't a smart thing to do. She shouldn't mix business and pleasure, but she had no way of stopping her body. Not now.

"This is my place. Adam's Morgan is just around the corner," he said, pointing down the street. Harrison took her hand and led her up the steps. Before he unlocked the lobby door, he kissed her. Their lips mashed together, tongues searching, exploring each other.

He somehow managed to put the key into the lock with his eyes closed and fully engaged in a kiss. Chloe was trying to get her hands under his shirt when they both jolted forward. The door gave and they tumbled into the hallway. They landed against the mailboxes and he kissed her deeply, his hands running down her body. He didn't stop even as he led her with his mouth towards his front door, leading to his apartment, leading to his bed.

Harrison stopped to get the right key. His chest heaved from heavy breathing. He unlocked the door and held it open. Chloe sashayed in, and Harrison gave her a playful smack on her bottom. She twirled in surprise, about to say something, but instead, he slammed the door and pinned her up against the wall.

He lifted her blouse up trying to take it off, but it got stuck. He yanked it down and fumbled with the tiny buttons. He slid it off her shoulders until it hung on her wrists, she flicked the shirt off and away into the darkness with wild abandon.

He pushed both hands against her breasts, pulled one breast free from her bra and took the nipple into his mouth. He lightly bit it and pinched the other nipple through her bra. She arched her back towards him, wanting more. He reached behind her and unclasped the bra freeing her breasts.

Chloe ran her hands underneath his shirt

exploring his muscled pectorals, lifted it over his head. They were chest to chest now, skin to skin. He hiked up her skirt. His hands caressed her round bottom. He found the back of her thong and pulled up. The fabric moved so it was taut against her slit. She jumped a little, the thong a source of aching pleasure.

He looked at her with ravenous need. He brushed his other hand over the front of her underwear. He pressed the lace against her heat and circled her clit with his thumb. The friction from the panties was incredible, and she rocked her hips back and forth, wanting the underwear gone, wanting him, pushing herself hungrily against him.

She tried pulling her underwear off, but he stopped her. She opened her eyes, and he shook his head. He raised her hands up over her head, pinning them against the wall with one of his. With his free hand, he traced the line of her neck, the curve of her breast, the swell of her belly--exploring every part of her before moving to her aching pussy. He palmed the lace of her thong against her mons, middle finger circling her clitoris.

She swallowed hard. She curled a leg around his hip, wanting him inside her. His fingers splayed her wide, the thong cutting into her folds. Chloe released a sigh as his finger entered her. She wanted more. More of him inside her. Now. She pushed against him hungrily.

"Harrison, I need you."

He released her arms and withdrew his hand from her wet, hungry pussy. He scooped her up under her thighs and she wrapped her legs around him. He pulled her tight against his chest Chloe wasn't even sure if they were going to make it to the bed, a mess of limbs and arms, kissing madly, but they did. He dropped her onto the mattress. She scooted back towards the headboard.

He pushed her thighs apart and knelt between her legs. She was naked and fully exposed.

"Harrison, I want you," she said, barely getting the words out through her raspy breath.

"Not yet Caiman," he said brusquely, and pushed the skimpy fabric to the side. He put two fingers inside her, slowly withdrawing them along her clit.

"More, please, Harrison, more..." She was desperate.

He picked up the pace, plunging his fingers deeper each time until they were pulsating inside her at a roughneck speed. She cried out again in pleasure, his fingers unrelenting against her throbbing heat. She lifted her hips up and towards him, her nipples pointed straight up in the air. Nothing else mattered to her right now but his touch. "Harrison, I can't wait. You have to."

"You'll wait, Caiman," he said to her, pressing up into her.

She was about to explode, her body wanted to let go. She cried out in anticipation, the pleasure building to heights she'd never known. The waves were about to come, a tsunami. She clamped her thighs around his hand, meeting his every thrust. He must have sensed how close she was.

"Not yet, Caiman." He pulled his fingers out and brought them up to his mouth, tasting her. "Sweet. Such a sweet little caiman."

She wanted to scream in frustration, she'd been so close.

Harrison pulled her thong off, freeing her at last. He pushed his thumbs into her, and splayed her labia open, revealing her completely to him. She relaxed her legs as he went down on her. His tongue darted in and out. He put her clit into his mouth and sucked, his bottom teeth raked against her heat. She clutched at his hair, needing to touch him somehow. His tongue, relentless now, taking her back to the brink of exploding ecstasy.

She threw her head back and clawed at the bedspread. She wanted to come, but she wanted to come with him inside her, it wasn't something she had ever experienced, but she just knew, she wanted it to be with him. "Harrison. I. Need. You. Now." Each word came out with a complete exhalation of breath—airy and hoarse.

"Not yet."

She almost screamed in frustration as he got off the bed. She rose up on her elbows in disbelief. How could he not fuck her? Then, she realized he still had his pants on. He took his sweet time unbuttoning and unzipping his pants, pulling his briefs off with them to reveal his erect cock.

He was fairly long and thick as a barrel. She reached out for his dick as he climbed onto the bed, but he playfully batted her hand away. "Later."

She laid back down on the bed and spread her legs for him. He teased her, circling her clit with the tip of his cock, pressing it against her and sliding his length along her slit.

"I want to feel you first." He closed his eyes and pushed in a quarter of his length.

She gasped as he stretched her. She raised her hips, to take more of him in, but he kept her at bay.

"Tsk tsk, Caiman. On my command."

Harrison pulled out and Chloe exhaled at the loss of him. What now?

He rustled through his nightstand and found a condom. She thrust her hips towards him playfully. He rolled the condom down his cock.

"You're so tight. Are you ready Caiman?" he asked. He rubbed hard against her clit, a spasm of pleasure jolted through her.

"Yes, Harrison. Yes."

He pressed into her slowly, watching her expression carefully.

Chloe gasped as he widened her taut pussy, accepted his whole length one inch at a time. She curled her hips into him, wanting him deeper. This experience was nothing like anything she'd ever had before. He drew back slowly, as if testing her ability to take him in. She bit her lip and arched her back, inviting him to take her completely and wholly and without reservation.

He slammed into her. Back and forth, he thrust into her, heavy and sure, like the pounding of the ocean on sand. She moaned with pleasure. She lifted a leg up over his shoulder, letting him in deeper, hungrily wanting more.

"Come Caiman! Come now!"

She put her hands on the backboard and met

him for every stroke, moaning louder. His length pulsed inside her. Her throbbing walls squeezed him tighter. The rhythm was animalistic, both of them bucking without abandon. She cried out as waves of ecstasy washed over.

His body shuddered in his final thrust. They collapsed on top of each other. Chloe had no words, she was still trying to catch her breath. Harrison breathed heavily too, his chest rising and falling.

Now she knew; she understood why people fell in love, why someone would stay married for fifty years, and why lovers killed.

"You. You are a feisty one." He brushed the hair behind her ears. "And you. You are all mine, Caiman."

Chloe smiled back. "Harrison. Um. I don't know how to say this, but, that was my first orgasm."

He kissed her and cradled her cheeks. "Me? Really? Never before?"

"Not like that. I, it's so weird, I want to cry and laugh at the same time."

"I'm honored darlin'. I want to make you happy."

She smiled, *happy*. "You are," she said playfully pinching his nipple, "making me happy."

He brought her into a hug. "I'm not letting you go Caiman. Not ever."

She burrowed into his chest, closing her eyes and inhaling his smell. "I'm right here." She couldn't believe the scale of her orgasm. Now she understood what her friends were talking about, why everyone wanted to have sex. She felt satisfied at her core, completely relaxed.

"Let me get you something to drink. Ice water?" he asked.

"Yes. That sounds perfect," she said. He stood up naked. He was glorious--strong muscles, V-shaped back, muscled thighs, his gorgeous ass. He was built like a quarterback.

As soon as she was alone, an unwelcome thought popped into her head.

What about Vegas?

Chapter 13

They slept together curled up in each other's arms. Chloe woke up early, and before she could get out of bed, Harrison pulled her back into the warmth of their little nest.

"Where do you think you're going? Call in sick to work."

"I wish. If we didn't have this crazy project coming up, I would."

"It is a crazy project. I'm glad you're on it."

"Me too. I just wish. Oh Harrison, I just wish I could go to Vegas. I wish I could go on my own merit and not... er, I mean." She halted the sentence, not wanting to tell him about the BINGO game, not wanting to expose the possibility of losing him.

"Maybe you can go. Who knows?" He nuzzled

her neck. "You smell so good." His hand moved under the sheets and cupped her breast.

"I have to work, Harrison."

His hand glided down between her legs. She was already wet.

"What is this? I swear, you are always ready for me."

"Something for you to remember me by," Chloe said, slipping out of bed. She wanted to satisfy her need, but she was already late. If it was anyone else but the Congressman, she would have called in sick and stayed naked with him all day long.

"I'm coming to get you after work. Immediately after work. And Friday too. Pack your bag Caiman, you're staying with me for the weekend."

"Ok," she said with a flirty smile, "If you insist." She dressed in her clothes from the night before. "How do you like my outfit? The walk of shame."

"There's no walk of shame, not with me. Besides, I like your outfit better when it's off." He flicked the covers off to reveal his erection. "Not a chance you get to leave. I don't care if you're meeting the president."

She leaned over the bed and wrapped her hands around his hard penis. "Oh? What do you want to do?"

He grabbed her shoulders and tossed her back onto the bed. Without hesitating, he thrust her skirt up to reveal her naked pussy. He groaned at the sight.

He grabbed a condom, tore it open, and rolled it down. She angled her hips up to meet him.

Harrison closed his eyes and sunk himself deep into her. "Oh my god, I love the feel of you." He rocked his hips hard against her.

She didn't know it was possible to come so fast, but she gasped in sharp bursts followed by an intense orgasm. It didn't have the earth-shattering intensity after the repeated build-up of the night before, rather it was it's own thing. Hard. Fast. Satisfying. A true quickie.

He came soon after, his manhood throbbing with release, his chest thrust forward, and then he collapsed on her.

"That's one way to say goodbye," she said, breathing hard.

"Sassy girl," he replied, lifting himself out of her, and giving her a kiss. "Off to work you go. Shit. I almost forgot ... Tonight, let's talk about what Gordy said."

CHLOE WAS saddle sore from the night before and adjusted her stride accordingly, acutely aware she was naked under the short skirt. She imagined him as he filled her up, all the way to the base of his cock, every velvety hard inch of him. And the orgasms. The one last night had been life-altering. The one this morning surprising in its rushed simplicity. Holy mackerel. Her breath caught just thinking about it. They were going to see each other again tonight. She sat down carefully on the Metro. Every uncomfortable moment was a reminder that she'd see him soon, and the soreness would turn into pleasure.

"I need to focus." She glanced around the train, hoping no one had heard her outburst. At home, she showered, wishing she didn't have to wash off the last of his lingering scent. She was unsure of what her evening plans were with Harrison, but she figured it would likely end with more sex. She put on her sexiest demi-cup lace bra and matching lace panties. *No thong burn tonight.* She covered them with office wear--a black fitted skirt and a black and white flowered blouse.

What would Harrison say about Gordy and his offer of a position at Porter and Associates? They clearly did not have a chance to talk about what happened last night, and this morning, well, there was no opportunity to talk either. She smiled at the memory of his kisses, his touch.

But when she thought about Gordy, she abruptly frowned. Gordy made it pretty clear to Harrison that they would offer her a job. What would she say? She didn't even know what she wanted herself. Sure, she loved Congressman Pierce, but shouldn't she be looking out for her own career? Wasn't her plan to work for a Congressman and then become a lobbyist. Her career goals had been so clear cut before, but now she wasn't sure.

Once at the Cannon office building, she skipped going to Link's office and headed to the Conference room for one of Katherine's early meetings. Chloe vowed that someday, when she was in charge, there would be no early morning meetings, ever. Katherine and Madeline were already inside sipping at their coffees, work spread out on the table.

Katherine waved Chloe inside. "Come in. Link's not coming to this one. We're just waiting for Harrison and then we'll start the meeting."

Chloe's mouth dropped. She was so glad that both Katherine and Madeline were busy on their phones. She collected herself. Why didn't he tell her he would be there? She grumbled. This was one reason having sex with co-workers was a bad idea.

Harrison opened the door. A brief smile crossed his lips as their eyes met, and then he looked away.

This was weird. Was he trying to collect himself? Was he feeling as awkward as she was?

When he faced her again, his expression was one of stoicism. There was no sign of acknowledgment.

What the hell? Was he just being a jerk, pretending to have nothing to do with her?

"Hi Katherine, Madeline. Chloe," he said without looking at her.

They waved a greeting to them, but neither of the other two women had looked up from their phones yet. Chloe was still half-asleep and in shock that he was at the meeting. Why hadn't he told her he'd be there? Chloe narrowed her eyes at him.

He sat down and slid a packet of papers to Katherine. She was still on her phone, so he busied himself with the paperwork. She decided to match him and put a professional expression on her face as well. Tit for tat.

Why did he say it like that?

"Thanks Harrison. Let's start off with a status report and then we'll get to the specifics," she said tapping his paperwork. "Chloe. You're up first."

"I'm working with Eleanor to gather additional background and precedence. I'm also reviewing the current status of various Oil and Gas bills coming thru both House and Senate. They'll be ready tomorrow."

"Great work. Harrison, once Chloe's finished you two meet up again," Katherine said and looked at Harrison. "Did you take care of Gordy?"

"We shut Gordy down," Harrison said, glancing towards Chloe with a neutral expression. "I doubt he'll keep sniffing around, but you never know with him. He's a stickler sometimes, so I'll keep my eye on him."

Embarrassed, Chloe blushed beat red. "Yes. Gordy is shut down."

What is he talking about? Gordy offered me a job, why didn't he tell Katherine and Madeline? He ignores me in the conference room, and then talks about protecting me from Gordy like I'm a business transaction? Does everyone know about us?

Chloe wasn't sure what to think about him now. What had just happened? It was like nothing had happened between them last night. Or this morning. Maybe she should forget about the whole thing, him, the sex, and focus on winning BINGO.

The team finalized some information and added 'Action Items.' Madeline reviewed her PR strategy. In less than an hour, the meeting wrapped up. Chloe wouldn't even look at Harrison. *Two can play this game.*

Madeline quickly gathered her things and left the room. Harrison seemed to take his time. She heard him gather his papers and place them in his briefcase. Then he stood up and left. She watched his backside go.

Only three hours before, that ass was naked, and now it was out the door. Vegas. She shouldn't have lost focus on the prize. As loathsome as it was to her, she decided to seriously consider Krista's offer to meet, maybe she would be better off on the lobbyist side of the fence. The grass sure seemed greener over there.

"Chloe," Katherine said, shaking her from her thoughts, "before you go, here's a constituent letter that Link wrote. He signed it personally, please make sure it gets out today."

"Course." Chloe took the letter without looking at it.

"I will be offsite for the rest of the day. I have some off-site prep for the hearing next week."

"Sure. Can I ask you something?"

Katherine stopped and looked like she would say *no.* Instead, she took a deep breath as if she were willing patience, "Yes?"

"I have to tell you what happened last night, at the Capital Bar. Gordy was there, he kept trying to hit on me. Almost kissed me, but Harrison stepped in."

"What? Do I need..." Katherine paused and thought for a moment. The tone of her voice changed. "Never mind. Great. That should throw Gordy off the scent."

"Er. There's more. Harrison and I ..."

Katherine put her hand up. "Wait one minute. Did you have sex with him or did you two just flirt?"

"Um." Chloe looked down and wanted to answer, but her face and neck bloomed bright red.

"I understand. Okay. So...Why are you upset?" she asked.

Chloe perked up. She was taken off guard by this response. "This sounds dumb, but last night I slept with him and now he's ignoring me."

Katherine shook her head slowly, her eyes narrowing on Chloe. "It didn't seem like that to me. He's probably just trying to maintain a professional demeanor, Chloe. Really. Let it go. I wouldn't read anything into it."

"You're right. Of course you're right. It's just work."

"I'm glad you told me though. This bill is important and our whole office is working hard to make sure it's a success." Katherine smiled kindly. "Don't let your romantic head get in the way, okay? We need you on board."

There was a knock on the conference room door, but before Katherine or Chloe could say a word, Carleen walked in.

"Hello ladies. I trust you're settling in, okay, Chloe?" she asked as she sat at the table. She said it with the same disinterest checkers at the grocery store ask how your day is going.

"I am, thank you," Chloe said, looking nervously at Carleen then back at Katherine. She was Katherine's boss---often referred to as Congressman Pierce's right-hand man---and a tough woman. If Katherine was legendary on the hill, Carleen was mythical. Would Katherine tell Carleen about Harrison? Surely, they didn't discuss people's sex lives. She'd never know though; Katherine and Carleen had begun their conversation as if Chloe wasn't even there.

Chloe gathered her laptop and placed it in her briefcase. If she wanted to have a career in politics though, who she slept with wouldn't matter, but the quality of work she produced would. She needed to get her head out of romance and back into the real world.

BACK IN THE MAIN OFFICE, Chloe did exactly what she said she would. Her head down, she focused on the constituent letters, email, and the list of action Items. She worked right through lunch.

"Earth to Chloe! Come in Chloe!" Cheyenne knocked on her desk.

Chloe looked up to find her friend in a determined stance with her arms crossed.

"You are working way too hard. Come with me for a coffee break. I want to hear about last night."

She released a deep breath, unaware that she had been holding it in. Chloe wanted to finish her work, but she decided to go with Cheyenne. She needed to vent. "Sure. Okay."

At the coffee shop, Chloe led Cheyenne to a relatively private corner where they sat down. "I think I'm losing it."

Cheyenne responded by raising her coffee cup in a semi-circle as if to say continue. "What happened? You were practically in the middle of a fist fight with Gordy and Harrison. Then you left with him."

"Those two. Oh my god. And, um. Yeah, Harrison and I went home together." Chloe couldn't help but smile.

"Did you? Oh my god, you did. I would too. He's so hot. So what's the problem?"

"I don't know. I really like him. I mean *really* like him. We made plans to go out again, but this morning...we had a meeting together with Katherine and Madeline. He was very formal, almost cold."

"I'm sure it was nothing. He was probably being professional. You know ... work face, game face."

"Still doesn't feel good though, to have him practically be a different person around me. Especially so soon after. Maybe I should steer clear of him."

"Easy there. One second you like him, the next you're writing him off? Put on your big girl pants and talk to him. *Ask* him about the meeting. *Ask* him why he was dissing you. I'm sure he's a good guy. He doesn't have that reputation up here anyway."

Chloe sat up straighter. "He is supposed to meet me after work."

"That's a perfect opportunity. Just *ask*. Talk to the man. Be confident."

"Spot on. And then there's Gordy. The lobbyist."

Cheyenne held up a warning finger. "Steer clear of *him*. Hell, steer clear of all lobbyists. They target us all for information. Try to use us when they can. When we get back to the office, I'll show you the rest of them, the lobbyists. There's a website with all their pictures. It gets updated monthly as they come and go."

"That would have helped on day one, you know?"

"It's usually part of an intern's orientation. But, I forgot about it, sounds like everyone did." Cheyenne looked down at her coffee cup, turning it around a couple of times before continuing. "Sooooo, I have to ask. Do you want to be with Harrison? Are you out of the BINGO game?"

Chloe regarded her suspiciously, wondering if her advice came as a friend or if she was trying to knock her out of the competition to Vegas.

"I don't know if Harrison wants to be with me. I'm still going to play. We've only gone out once. It's not like we are exclusive." She shifted the conversation so they could stop talking about her and Harrison. "You're doing well! Three check-ins, right on the heels of Madeline. She has four now?"

"I think so. I kissed that cute guy from the first night. Meh. Got me my "B", right? And Peter was an okay kisser I guess. I have another date tonight to get me up to three. I'm hoping Katherine will hook me up with someone from the CIA for another one."

"CIA? That sounds adventurous. Madeline will probably go to Vegas. She's so close to winning."

"Not if I have anything to do with it," said Cheyenne, lifting up her coffee cup. "And you too. Let's do it, let's win this."

"Yeah," Chloe returned her cheers with a firm tap, but her voice had undertones of fake enthusiasm. "But only one of us can win."

"Let's just make sure it's not Madeline, okay? Want to go out Saturday night? Let's try a new place."

"We'll see. I want to see what happens with Harrison." Even though it had only been one night—one amazing beautiful fantastic over the moon night--the idea of being physical with anyone else repulsed her. She didn't want to kiss any other guys. But if she was going to play with the big dogs, if she wanted to go to Vegas, she needed to get her game on.

Chapter 14

Late afternoon, Chloe sat on the toilet. She didn't even have to go to the bathroom, she just wanted to be alone. She chose the stall furthest from the entrance. He hadn't called or texted all day. The stress of wondering about him caught up to her. She didn't want to cry, but all of a sudden, she couldn't handle it for one second more. She headed to the bathroom before she had a full meltdown right in the office.

What kind of professional am I? She didn't want to play BINGO, but she would, even if her heart wasn't into it. Tears sprung up. But she had to play, didn't she? To be successful. To get to Vegas. Chloe leaned forward trying to release the breath caught in her throat. Maybe she should just go to Krista and take that job offer.

She heard the door open. Swiftly, she stilled herself, pulled her feet up, and became very quiet. She didn't want anyone to know she was here, crying about a stupid boy. Like a school girl. God, she was a school girl. She didn't want them to know what a baby she was being.

She heard the clicking of high heels, two people. Neither individual went inside a stall, but stood in front of the mirror. Chloe peered out between the cracks of the stall door. It was Katherine and Cheyenne.

"What the fuck is going on with Chloe?" asked Katherine.

Cheyenne started to say something, and then looked behind her at the stalls. Chloe recoiled from the crack, holding her breath. Cheyenne walked to the first stall and opened the door. A second one. A third one.

Chloe heard her footsteps getting closer and instinctively raised her knees closer to her chest. Chloe would die if Cheyenne opened the door on her. She focused on the stall door in horror and held her breath. Cheyenne's pointy Louboutin's appeared under the stall door when Katherine spoke again.

"Come on. You are so over the top. All you have to do is look underneath. There is no one in here."

"Oh, fine. Whatever." Cheyenne spun away. "Actually, I'm worried about her. She's upset about Harrison. I don't want this project to get fucked up. But yeah, Chloe and Harrison did it. He's acting like an asshole now."

So Cheyenne did think he was an asshole. Why had she lied to her earlier?

"Chloe told me this morning that they'd slept together."

"She did?"

"Yes. After our morning meeting. Ugh. I wish Harrison would have kept his dick in his pants, what the hell was he thinking? I suggested he date her, not fuck her."

If only Chloe could see Cheyenne's face to gauge her reaction. Shit, Katherine was cold.

I only told him to date her, not fuck her.

Chloe leaned as close to the crack in the stall as she could, trying to see the other women's faces. Was she surprised that Katherine could be so calculating? Was Cheyenne in on this, too?

Cheyenne was quiet for a moment. "Should I say anything to her?" she asked at last, her voice quiet, tentative.

"Just tell her the truth. He's trying too hard to be a professional, he overshot his angle. That's all. No big deal. And it's the truth. He's here somewhere, he mentioned a meeting scheduled this afternoon."

"Can we trust him? I mean, is he a good guy? He's not like Gordy is he?"

"Harrison is gold." Katherine said with confidence. "I have to go. Are we good? They'll be fine." Katherine paused, "Hey, I appreciate you letting me know."

After both women left the room, Chloe put her feet on the ground. In shock, she still couldn't believe what she had heard. She opened the stall, washed her hands, and went back to her desk as if on automatic. On her way out, Chloe went from shock to outright anger.

Cheyenne? Why didn't she approach her first? And Katherine? She expected this kind of behavior from Madeline, but not Katherine. High holy hell, she planned to rip into Harrison next time she saw him. She stopped, and was intent on finding him, but she had no idea where he might be. Frustrated, she checked her phone. The no new messages ticked her off even more. *Fuck him.*

At her desk, she tried to dive into her workload, but the anger left her feeling like she wanted to punch a door. It was only 5:45 pm. He would be here to pick her up in fifteen minutes, but she didn't want to see him. If he even showed.

I only told him to date her, not fuck her.

On the verge of tears, Chloe held herself in check. Could she trust Katherine anymore? Or Cheyenne? Harrison? She shut her computer down and powered her phone off. She was going home.

Chapter 15

Chloe tossed on her summer jacket. She knew it was late enough the workmen had left the East end of the building. Maybe she could escape, unseen, through the renovations. She turned a corner toward the mostly abandoned hallways only to see him heading her direction.

The clean shaven strong jaw, his stride purposeful towards her.

As if he owned her. Hmpf.

She came to a halt, planting her feet side-by-side with a determined little stomp. She was totally going to give him a piece of her mind. She'd do it quietly, but with strength, in her own words.

He would have no confusion as to where she stood. The hallway zoomed out, her only focus was him, getting to him, and telling him to go straight to hell. She almost lost her nerve until she saw his eyes. They seemed to be laughing at her.

"Hey, Chloe. There you are, did you get lost?"

She crossed her arms. "Don't 'Hey Chloe' me." She spat the words out through clenched teeth. "So, Katherine ordered you to date me, is that it?"

He stepped back from her wrath, but stood his ground. "I don't take orders. If I wanted to date you it was because I wanted you."

"Was fucking me your plan or part of hers?" she asked menacingly.

"Listen here, Caiman," he said, his voice dropping to a calming lull. He stepped a little closer, his hand out palm down in a placating gesture. "If I did, it's because *I* wanted to. Not because of something Katherine said."

And now he's talking to me like a wild animal. Who does he think he is? A caiman whisperer?

She steeled her jaw, clenched her hands, and pushed back her shoulders.

He took a deep breath, "I want *you* Chloe. You. No one else. That's it. That's the truth. I'm sorry if I was cold this morning. I was just being professional."

After the last eight hours of worrying herself crazy, she refused to budge and continued her glare.

Harrison wouldn't break eye contact with her, but then, for a brief second, he glanced off to the side. There was construction going on in the building, massive renovations to replace all the electricity and plumbing in the century-old building. The entrance was draped in plastic sheeting. Harrison gave her that half mischievous, half innocent smile. He grabbed her with lightning quick speed, pulling her behind the sheeting.

"What are you doing?" she hissed, struggling to free herself, pulling against his grip. "We can't go in here."

Harrison didn't answer, but tightened his hand as he led her over scraps of wood and metal until they were deep inside the construction area and to an empty room stripped down to the studs.

"We need privacy. You look like you're going to blow up. Too many people can see us out there. Like Gordy," he said, gracing her with a 'you should know this' expression.

"Don't you dare look at me like that. Don't you treat me like some dumb intern."

"Don't play all innocent Miss Chloe." He placed his fingers in her hand and interlaced them, then squeezed and pressed down. The motion brought her closer to him, their faces were just an inch apart.

"Am I *just* part of your BINGO game? Am I *just* some pawn to you?"

Chloe's heart thudded. Her body strained toward him. She wanted to kiss him passionately, but held back. She had no idea he knew about the game. She leaned back to evaluate his expression. His face was set. She knew he wasn't bluffing.

"Katherine told you."

"Are you playing?"

Chloe swallowed hard. If there was any chance of her and Harrison having a decent relationship, she had to come clean.

"Yes. I want to go to Vegas, so I am playing BINGO. Was playing…"

"Have you kissed anyone else?"

"No. You were my first, my B. My only."

"I *was* your first, wasn't I?" he said with a grin. He leaned in to kiss her. His tongue pressed against her lips.

She didn't want to kiss him at first, he still had to pay for being so insensitive earlier, but she was help-less against his touch. She parted her lips as he pressed his mouth against her. His free hand pulled her to him. She responded in kind with a strong and aggressive kiss, until they were both panting. Her body hot against his.

Breathing hard, she pulled back.

"I still want to go to the meeting in Vegas. It will change my life, my career. Will you help me?"

"With one condition."

"Condition?" She searched his eyes for what might come next.

"No one else kisses you. You are done with the BINGO thing."

Chloe giggled with relief. That was easy. "That I can do."

"Don't worry about Vegas. I can't promise anything, but I think we might find a way to get you there. Do you trust me?"

"I trust you." In spite of the white-hot anger she'd been feeling minutes before, she did trust him. She more than trusted him. His spicy smell was like coming home. She wanted so badly to wrap her legs around him and have him take her away.

He kissed her again. She responded with her body, demanding him. He playfully pushed her body back against the door.

"Caiman. Steady."

He engulfed her wrists in one hand, pinning both on the wall above her head.

"You like this don't you?" she asked, touching

the top of her lip with her tongue. She could leave if she wanted to, but she didn't want to.

"I do, I can't get enough of you." He dipped towards her neck, licking and kissing her sensitive skin. With his free hand, he yanked up the fabric of her skirt to access her without having to let go of her hands. A well-muscled leg stepped between her legs. He lifted it until she was on her tippy toes and her wet pussy against his thigh. His eyes darkened when he realized she was soaked through her thin panties.

"Tsk tsk Caiman. I'm going to make sure you're mine." He brought his face in close and gave her nose a nuzzle before rubbing his stubble against her cheek.

"Say it Caiman. Tell me."

"Harrison, I want you." There was no other answer.

She wanted him inside her again, wanted his touch, craved it. She arched her back. His free hand flew to her breast. He untucked her shirt and pulled the cup of her bra down. With one smooth movement, he cupped the whole of her breast in his hand, squeezing it, but not taking the nipple. She was still precariously balanced on his knee, the slight movements causing ripples of ecstasy.

Chloe wanted to tell him to take her nipple, but

was overwhelmed with desire and unable to say anything. He moved his hands, over her waist and straight for her pussy. He pulled her panties aside roughly. His fingers massaged her clit. She moved her body towards him, her hips, wanting him more.

"Say it, darlin'." He dropped his foot and she put her feet on the ground, resting against the stud. She unzipped his pants. His member sprang forth. He was huge. Perfection.

Chloe wrapped her fingers around his cock, laying claim to him even as she spoke. "I'm yours, Harrison."

He lifted her chin. His brown eyes stared into hers. "Am I the only one?"

Chloe didn't answer right away. Harrison moved closer to her. He rubbed his stubble against her chin, and his finger found her clit, rubbing it back and forth. Desire ripped through her body, fresh wetness coated her clit. She moved her hips to match his rhythm, almost coming to climax.

"Tell me I'm the only one." He removed his hand from her. The motion jarred her. Frustrated her need.

She still didn't answer, her body stunned. He spread his fingers so her clit was exposed to the air. She shivered. Then he very lightly moved his finger across her clit again. The light movement caused her skin to break out into goose bumps, even the barest touch felt exquisite.

"Say it."

"You're the only one Harrison. My first and only one."

Harrison placed two fingers inside her, pressing up against her g-spot. Chloe let out a yelp in response. He pulled out of her and smelled his finger first, then put it in his mouth, "Sweetness."

He pushed the skirt up so it was around her waist, then lifted her against the door and held her. He guided himself inside her as gravity helped her slide down against his length.

She loved the way her opening stretched around him, the tightness a ring of pleasure, the way he slid inside her, spreading her apart, filling her. Her body squeezed him, instinctively pulling him closer.

"You fit me perfectly," he said before pulling back, almost imperceptibly, and thrust inside her.

She lifted her legs and locked them around his waist. She gripped him with her strong legs and he pounded into her. She squeezed inside herself, matching him.

He plunged deeper. She moaned and pressed her head against the doorframe. She stiffened and knew it was coming. He pummeled deep inside her again and again.

She swore he was touching her core, touching her very essence. She felt the tight squeeze release from her body and wave after wave flowed through her.

He shuddered and his last push went in up to his root. Waves kept flowing through her, up and out of her.

He gently held her against the door, spent. In between his breaths, he whispered, "I am yours."

Harrison gently released her. She stepped to the ground, wobbly. He helped to steady her. "Caiman. Let's go to my place."

"Aren't you done yet?" she asked, incredulous.

"Not by a long shot Caiman. I'm just getting started. Let's go home. We'll stop by your house first, so you can pack a bag. I think you'll be staying awhile."

Chloe nodded. With a shy smile, she gave him a kiss on the cheek. He took her hand, closed his eyes, and pressed it against his cheek.

Chapter 16

Friday morning, Harrison kissed Chloe goodbye and watched her head out the door for Capitol Hill. He turned and headed for the shower. Normally, Harrison did not mix work and romance. There was too much to risk, especially in DC. He had seen one too many jilted lovers ruin aspirations out of spite. Not that Chloe was that way, even with her playing the game, he could sense that she cared about him, that this kind of game playing wasn't her nom de guerre.

This was a temporary project for the both of them, and it was over in a matter of weeks, a month if she went to Vegas with the team. Harrison believed their relationship would be safe from the difficulty of mixing strong emotions and a professional atmosphere. Did it matter though? They were already in too deep, he couldn't step back. He didn't want to. At the office, they would be kind and cordial to one another, but they would under no circumstances be public with their affection.

His first meeting of the day was with Katherine to give her a status report on the upcoming bill. Harrison headed to the conference room Katherine had scheduled. He planned to ask her about Chloe, to see if she could be part of the team that went to Vegas. If she said no though, would he try to force her hand? Would he use the BINGO game against her?

The question had been on his mind since last night. If he did try to force her hand, the good working relationship he had built over the years with Katherine would be over. Even though he and Katherine had never dated, he considered her an ally in this harsh world of politics. How far would he go for Chloe?

Once in the conference room, he sat down. Harrison looked out the arched window and into an internal courtyard of a park like area. Every room in the house has a good view, at least, that was the idea. Even so, the style still surprised him, where he grew up, buildings didn't have a courtyard in the center.

Katherine came into the room. She set up across the table from him, and pulled out her laptop, a notebook, and a Montblanc pen. She hadn't said anything to him, she was obviously ensconced in her own thoughts.

He didn't want to disturb her just yet, given that he was about to ask her something incredibly sensitive. The last thing he wanted was to annoy her by interrupting her train of thought. He checked his smartphone for any new messages, and felt a twinge of guilt. He still hadn't sent a text to Chloe yet, his day had been just packed, running from one meeting to the next. He moved from the window to his seat.

She looked up at him in surprise, "Oh! You're here already. I didn't even see you."

"You were busy thinking about something, or someone?"

She smiled and raised one of her eyebrows. "Let's get started shall we?"

"Before we get too far into our edits, I wanted to talk to you about Chloe."

Katherine didn't answer. Normally, her facial expressions were poker worthy, but he saw her tighten her lips just briefly, before her expression returned to its normal cool and unreadable state.

"Alright then. I'll go right ahead and ask. As you

know, she's been doing phenomenal work. Normally, we don't have an intern working on these kinds of projects, but well, we had to improvise. She's come up with some great edits and new ideas. With that, we should bring her along to the Vegas meetings. We're going to need her there."

Katherine leaned back in her chair and rubbed at her temples with her fingertips and closed her eyes. After a while, she sighed and clasped her hands in front of her and placed them on the table. "No can do Harrison. We just can't. I want to. I want all of us to go, but only one of us can. If we send an intern to Vegas, do you know how many people will be looking at us? Do you realize how many eyes will be on us?"

"What if I have my office pay for her trip? What if she is working as my liaison?"

"It's against the law to have you pay for her trip. But she could quit her internship here and work for you."

Harrison thought about that, but having someone he was dating as his intern was a bad idea. "Come on Katherine. You need her in Vegas."

"There's nothing I can do Harrison. In fact, it has crossed my mind. I want at least two people to go because of the extra workload. Whoever goes will have to work incredibly hard. There's a lot to cover. But if she goes to Vegas on Pierce's team, Gordy and Krista will be all over us. If you take her down there, we're breaking the law. But talk to her, if she wants to quit and work for you, I wouldn't like it, but I'd absolutely give her a glowing recommendation."

Harrison almost mentioned the fact that Katherine had asked him to date Chloe. That Katherine used subterfuge to keep this project under wraps. He could easily sway her decision about bringing Chloe to the SUNFLOWER meetings, but even if Chloe did go, Katherine was right, it would raise the hackles of every single lobbyist. He wanted this project to be successful, it would be one of the first meetings between standard industry and renewables, something he'd worked for since he started college. He still had time, exactly seven days to be exact. And Chloe should be the one to decide. After all, it was her career.

"I'll talk to Chloe then. Either of us will get back to you."

"Tick-tock Harrison. I'll need to know as soon as possible."

Chapter 17

Friday at the office couldn't pass soon enough. Chloe had been texting all afternoon with Harrison about their plans, which were finalized to cook dinner at his place and then go to a movie. Madeline left early to leave for her sister's and Katherine was, well, she didn't know, but she wasn't in the office. No one was in the office for that matter. Chloe had finished her work, so she grabbed her work briefcase, overnight bag and headed to Harrison's.

After she changed into some jeans and a t-shirt, she came into the kitchen. A glass of wine waited for her.

"I love this wine Harrison. What is it?" Chloe asked holding a wine glass filled with white wine up to the light. It was golden and bright. She swirled it around and inhaled a citrusy aroma. "Mmm. I love it."

Harrison was in his office finishing up the last of his work, and he called out, "the bottle is in the fridge. I got it from Madeline a few days ago, her Dad has that winery in Napa Valley."

Chloe took it out of the fridge and set it on the counter. She didn't like wine to be too cold. "That's right. Madeline's Dad is in town, and he brought up a few cases to the office. I picked out some Cabernets and a couple whites. I hope I have this one."

"I've never been to a winery. Never been to California," he said.

"We should go. A winery in Napa Valley. It's super romantic. Her dad is hoping to attract big weddings. Madeline showed me pictures. It looks like a Tuscany villa. Maybe they do a stomping of the grapes? That would be fun."

"I could see you doing that. I'll be out in a minute to start dinner. Spicy Cajun shrimp."

Chloe set her glass down on the breakfast bar. His kitchen was small, but it was designed for a chef. There was a Viking gas stove with an overhang fan. Part of the counter was a refurbished butcher's block made from reclaimed wood from the Cannon Building, and the countertops were gorgeous quartz. The man had style, that was for sure.

Everything about him was perfect. She was falling for him, harder than she anticipated. The memory of his kisses at work flashed by and she smiled. *At work!* A sigh came over her. She rubbed her jaw with uncertainty.

She wanted to ask him what happened at work, specifically what happened during his meeting with Katherine. The meeting had happened at 10:30 that morning, and he hadn't texted any results. She didn't want to bug him about it, but she was dying of suspense. She swallowed hard and decided the direct way would be the best way.

"Harrison...soooo...What happened at the meeting today? Are we going to Vegas? Am *I* going to Vegas?"

The slight tapping of computer keys stopped. She heard him shut the laptop and within a minute he had joined her. He still wore his business clothes for the day, but had loosened up his tie. He ran a hand from the back of his neck and up through his thick wavy curls.

Chloe sat on a stool. He stood between her legs. He brushed a long strand of her brown hair back, and kissed her on the forehead. Then he stepped back and went into the kitchen. He got out a glass and poured himself some wine.

"I talked to Katherine this morning. I wanted to talk to you, but things went haywire at the office today. Besides, I needed to talk to you face to face."

"What did she say?" Chloe clasped her hands to keep them from getting too jittery.

"There are a couple options Caiman. You'll get to decide," he said and sipped some of the wine. "If you want to go to Vegas, you'll have to quit your job and come work for me. I can hire you on as a temp, and you'll go to Vegas to help me. When we get back we can see about you coming on a more permanent position."

"What's the other option?" asked Chloe, unable to hold back her enthusiasm.

"You stay an intern with Pierce, but unless you are selected as the one to go to Vegas, you don't go to Vegas."

The possibility was there, to work with Harrison, but they were ...

"There's a caveat."

"What's that"

"If you come to work for me, we have to stop dating."

"And if I stay as an intern, I don't get to go to Vegas."

"That's it. That's your decision. I can't date anyone I work with, I won't do it. It's not fair to you darlin' and it's not good business."

"You're kidding right? I mean, this temp position would only be for a week, until SUNFLOWER is over. It's not like I'm working for you."

"But you are. Listen," he said, returning to her side, "I don't want to risk losing you, but I've worked damn hard as a lawyer. That's why I'm giving you choices."

"What would you do if you were me?"

"It's a hard decision Chloe, but you've got to make this one on your own. Pros and cons list is a good start."

"Come on Harrison. Help me out."

"Look Chloe. There are plenty of professional opportunities that will come up." He got out a sauté pan from underneath the stove and set it on top. He opened up the fridge and retrieved a plastic bag of tiger shrimp, "Like Gordy's opportunity. Did he offer you something at Porter and Associates?"

Chloe looked out the window and over the grove of tall oaks. She didn't want to answer his question, but she knew she had to, she knew she had to decide.

"I did get a soft offer from Gordy and Krista. She wanted me to call her if I was interested in joining the team."

"And are you? Interested?" he asked, he put the bag of shrimp in the sink and turned on the hot water to defrost them a bit.

"To be honest, I kind of am. They offered a lot of money. I am a hundred and eighty thousand dollars in debt. And I am interning. How the fuck am I going to do this? It'd be stupid not to take the job."

"I get that. I was in the same position when I finished grad school. Gordy needed to make money so he can stay in the Richie Rich club. I cared more about what I do every single day. That I could respect myself at the end of the day."

"That's what it all comes down to, right. What do I really want?"

"What do you want?"

"I want to help," said Chloe, standing up. She came into the kitchen. "Where's the colander?"

"Under there," he said pointing. "It's in the back, a wire mesh one."

Chloe bent down and dug in the cabinet. She found the colander. When she stood up, she found Harrison gazing at her, admiring her body.

"I remember the first time we met," said Harrison, "wasn't too long ago Caiman. And ever since that moment, you never cease to amaze me. You're downright beautiful."

Her stomach fluttered. She felt at home with him, so comfortable and natural. "For your own sake Harrison, then you better hope I decide to stay an intern with Pierce."

"I hope you do. I'm not giving you up."

"Would you?"

"Don't make me answer that. It's company policy. I did break the rules once, and it didn't go well, at all. While I trust you, I will never do it again. It's just my rule. Firm as a marble statue's backside."

"I'll need time to figure out what I want."

"Katherine's waiting for your decision by Monday."

After dinner, Chloe and Harrison went to a movie. It was a sci-fi movie with lots of special effects and loud noises---a guy movie--- but they held hands through the whole thing, his leg rested comfortably against hers. They shared popcorn and even a straw for the drink.

While he watched the movie, she looked at him,

studied him. What was he to her? Everything he said to her, she believed him, everything about him felt right. Sometimes love was just as hard to find as a great job. But love seemed harder.

Love was a hay bale of fate stacked on top of another: he was the right guy who wasn't on a rebound, having just broken up with someone. He was ready for a relationship, he liked her, he didn't annoy her. And she was the right girl too, ready to be in a new relationship.

They were attracted to each other. They had great sex. They lived in the same town, she was only a ten-minute cab ride away. Love was just as difficult to find considering the crucial timing that had to occur. Should she trust that love would work out? Should she trust in Harrison? Or should she focus on getting to Vegas?

The opportunity in Vegas was an insane chance that might never come twice. She lucked out on this internship that others had worked every contact they had. She had a chance to meet Yukika and August, who were premier entrepreneurs of alternative energies. She might not ever get this chance again. Going to Vegas was a game changer for her professional career. It might never happen again.

Chloe ground her teeth. She wanted both. She

wanted Harrison to be her boyfriend, and she wanted to go to Vegas. But that option wasn't available. She had to choose between Harrison or Vegas.

Frustrated, she crossed her legs and stared at the movie with its swashbuckling and easy choices. She had to make a decision. Even though she had time, realistically, she'd have to make one by morning. She didn't want to lead Harrison on either.

After the movie, they walked home. Chloe would later recall she didn't know the exact thing that helped to make up her mind. It might have been the way the evening breeze warmed her skin. Maybe it was the shadow of the tree leaves under a street lamp. It could have been the romantic jazz she heard in the streets coming from a musician playing on the sidewalk for money. When they got home, he tilted her chin up and kissed her on the front steps. She looked into his eyes and found herself lost in the brown earthiness.

His smell, with its peppery high notes, comforted her, but still—she bit her top lip. She hadn't felt this way in a long time. Jack, the love of her life in high school seemed like a childish rendition of what she felt when she was with Harrison.

He bent down and kissed her softly on the lips. His arms wrapped around her and brought her in close. His tongue parted her lips and explored her mouth. Her hands reached up and into his hair. Her thumbs massaged a point right below his ears.

He stopped kissing her. Holding her hands, he stepped back, their arms swung between them. "You coming with me, Caiman?"

A simple question, really.

Without a word---nothing clever came to mind---she let go of one hand, stepped forward and stood next to him.

"Yes."

He placed his hand on her cheek. "Yes?"

"Yes," she repeated, a little louder and more sure sounding.

Harrison gave a little whoop and took her hand. They went into his condo and skipped over the kitchen, past the living room, and headed straight for the bedroom.

"Wait here," he said. Once inside the room, he put on soft music and lit a few candles. He flicked off the light switch. Standing next to her, he held her hand in his.

"I'm glad you chose to stay with me," he said.

"I am too."

Without taking his eye off her, Harrison lifted

off her shirt, slowly. He pulled down her jeans, then stood back to admire her.

"All of you. So beautiful, Caiman. I want to see you."

She returned his gaze with a sultry smile. Reaching behind her she unclasped her bra and let it fall to the ground. She saw him swallow heavily, but he didn't move towards her. Next, she clipped the edges of her panties with her thumb and pulled them down, off her body. His eyes widened, and they were intense, on her.

He stood up and kissed her intently. Gone was the animalistic passion from before, and here was a man who regarded her, who wanted and craved her. His hand cupped her round breast, the weight heavy in his hand. He turned her and laid her down on the bed.

Slowly, silky, like a cat, he moved on top of her, and kissed her belly, then her belly button. His hand moved down to her slippery folds. He parted them and began to rhythmically push her clit. He kissed her mound. Once down there, he used his fingers to pull her apart and just stayed still, looking into her.

She knew he could see her, the very core of her and knew everything.

Her body clenched in response and then she relaxed. She let her knees fall apart, opening to him. He licked one side of her and with his hand stretched her opening. His tongue teased her clit with flicking lashes. She tried to move his head, but he shook her off. Then, he repeated his actions on the other side. One long lap on the side of her opening, his fingers pressed firmly inside of her, and his tongue flicked against her clit.

He sat back again. Surely he could see how much she wanted him, surely he saw that she belonged to him. He sat up on his knees and raised her hips to him. Her feet flat on the bed, she raised her hips high in the air to meet him, a bridge pose in yoga.

He cupped her buttocks, lifting her higher and his mouth dove into her, taking her hungrily, sucking hard on her clit, lapping her over and over. His mouth took her fully and sucked until she was throbbing. Spasms came through her, her body thrust harder and harder against him, but still she was unsatisfied.

It wasn't enough to have him lick and touch her, she wanted his full length inside her, to touch her core.

"Harrison! I ... oh god, Harrison!"

"Hold on, Caiman, hold on."

"Please, oh god, I have to have you now."

He lowered her hips. Once she was flat on the bed, he pushed her knees apart and slipped on a condom. She felt his tip right at her opening and he paused for a moment, just as he always did.

She looked up at him and their eyes locked on each other. He pushed into her, falling into her almost. She stretched open to receive him with a pleasant sigh until he was all the way in.

His body pressed against hers. Back and forth, they settled into a rhythmic pulse to satiate both of their instinctive, deep hunger. Together, they thrust into each other until wave after wave flew threw her. Just before his final thrust, he burrowed his head into her breast and held her close.

She threw her arms around him, not wanting to ever let him go. She was home.

More by Juno Chase

The DC Knights series can be read in any order, but we hope you don't miss any of them!

New to the Game—D.C. Knights Book 1

Chloe's the new intern, but she jumps into the game both feet first.

Playing For Keeps—D.C. Knights Book 2

Katherine thinks she's got things figured out until a sexy scientist tangos his way into her heart.

All In—D.C. Knights Book 3

Madeline has no problem playing games until she meets Ewan a man who knows how to treat her like a woman.

Fair and Square—D.C. Knights Book 4

Lizbeth doesn't have time for games, but she ends up in the midst of a political game no one in Congressman Pierce's office saw coming.

Only Bluffing—D.C. Knights Book 5

Eleanor Winslow and Daniel Prado are from different worlds. Will their love overcome dark histories and ancient legacies?

Game On—D.C. Knights Book 6

Cheyenne LeFleur lives on the wild side. Will Alexander Moore be able to handle her history, or will he reject her like so many before him?

For the Win—D.C. Knights Book 7 The final chapter in this series. Congressman Lincoln Pierce deserves love, too. Can he find it while maintaining his principles?

Also by Juno Chase:

ARTIFACT of BETRAYAL: an exciting romantic suspense novel

If you had to choose between saving your life or the love of your life, *who would you choose?*

Claire Townsend has it all, a great job, her own shop in Brooklyn, until one night when she loses everything. With thirteen days to pay off a dangerous loan shark, she decides to partake in a black-market smuggling operation to save her own neck.

Bruno Canul is an archeologist who works as a consultant

with the FBI. He chases a suspect to Belize only to find the ex-love-of-his-life as part of the crew. He can't tell if he should trust Claire or if she's joined forces with the smuggler.

Afraid her choices will get Bruno killed, Claire tries to resist falling back in love with him. If she goes through with the smuggling scheme, she can pay off her loan, but she'd lose Bruno's love and trust *forever*. If she stands up for their love, she's a dead woman.

This adventurous romantic suspense is sure to keep you on the edge of your seat as Claire and Bruno find love in the jungle and ancient Mayan ruins of Belize.

About Juno Chase

Who said chivalry is dead? They were totally wrong! We love, love, love hot guys who are modern day knights and heroes but also know how to heat things up between the sheets.

Juno Chase is the nom de plume of two married moms who love reading and writing happy stories. We wanted to see these modern day knights celebrated in romance, so here we are. We're not a big group of people writing—there is just the two of us. We both spend lots of time reading and writing in each story to bring you the most complete, hot, and exciting stories possible.

Thank you so much for reading *New to the Game*, we hope you enjoyed reading it as much as we did writing it. If you sign up for our newsletter, you will be the first to know whenever we have a new book available.

Follow Juno Chase on your favorite social Media.
We'd love to hear from you!

www.Junochase.com
juno@junochase.com

Acknowledgments

We'd like to thank a few people who helped us get this book into your lovely hands, dear readers. We are part of an amazing writing group who has listened to our ideas, helped us with plotting, and given us some straight feedback. We couldn't have done this without your energy and help-—you ladies rock! Thank you for all your reading time and thoughtful suggestions to help make the D.C. Knights series a reality.

To our intrepid beta readers. Thank you for taking the time to read and give us honest criticism. Especially to Dawn who has faithfully read everything we've handed her and keeps asking for more! And to our families—our fabulous husbands and children who have supported us in so many different ways and picked up the pieces as needed. We love you!

www.ingramcontent.com/pod-product-compliance
Lightning Source LLC
Chambersburg PA
CBHW050529190726